To THE C[...]
OF DEC[...]

CW00796231

ALL BEST WISHES

DON'T
FORGET
TO BREATHE

PS: DON'T FORGET

To READ IT :)

B. D. W[...]

23.7.24

Published in paperback in 2023 by Sixth Element Publishing
on behalf of Steven David Wood

Sixth Element Publishing
Arthur Robinson House
13-14 The Green
Billingham
TS23 1EU
www.6epublishing.net

ISBN 978-1-914170-42-3

British Library Cataloguing in Publication Data. A catalogue record for this book is
available from the British Library.

Steven David Wood asserts the moral right to be identified as the author of this work.

Printed in Great Britain.

DON'T FORGET TO BREATHE

STEVEN DAVID WOOD

This book is dedicated to Pamela,
without whom it would not exist. x

Also, to my Mam and Dad,
without whom I would not exist. x

And to all my family and friends,
both present and absent. x

PART 1
SANDY BEACHES AND RUSTY NAILS

PROLOGUE

Sometimes things get lost at sea. Sometimes for days, weeks, months, even for millions of years. Then sometimes, those things get washed up on the shoreline and a person will come along and pick one of them up and take it home. Sometimes these discoveries happen by accident, and sometimes they happen for a reason. This is the story of a beachcomber, and his name is Andrew Teach.

He was in his fifties, and as he shuffled along the familiar beach, pulling the old shopping trolley behind him (not the kind at Tesco but the type favoured by old ladies to transport their shopping home), something caught his eye in the bed of small pebbles on the sand at his feet. He bent down and picked it up. It was a small old-fashioned key like the type you might use to open an ancient door, but it seemed to be in remarkably good condition. He scrutinised it like it was a piece of treasure then put it in his pocket. Thinking of treasure made him recall a story that his father had told him when he was a boy… apparently, his family, on his father's side, was related to a man called

Edward Teach, a famous pirate of the 1700s, who also went by the name Blackbeard. He was brought up in Bristol but operated around the West Indies and Britain's North American colonies, terrorising the local shipping using what was a former slave ship that he had stolen from the French and renamed Queen Anne's Revenge. He would put lit fuses in his hair to enhance his fearsome appearance, unnerving his opponents even more than his reputation did. Eventually though, he was killed by the Royal Navy in November 1718 during a ferocious battle, his head being cut off and suspended from the bowsprit of one of their sloops for all to see. The surviving members of his crew were all hung along the side of a street, which gained the name of the Gallows Road.

Andrew felt that he had a connection with Blackbeard because of his constant enthusiasm for scouring the local beach for treasure, although it wasn't the kind of plunder that the pirate would have been pursuing. Andrew's idea of treasure was the likes of fossils, unusual seashells, pieces of broken coloured glass that had been smoothed by the action of the waves, broken pieces of crockery and anything else unusual that caught his eye. The tide came in and out twice a day and about an hour later each day. When the high tide had ebbed sufficiently and the weather and daylight permitted, Andrew would slowly walk the high tide line, scanning carefully in all directions a few feet around himself, hoping to discover some interesting artefacts.

CHAPTER 1
1960s AND 1970s

Andrew's parents, Jim and Iris, had bought a small cottage on Cliff Drive in Marske-by-the-Sea shortly after they were married in the mid-1960s. Marske is situated on the North East coast of England, between Redcar and Saltburn-by-the-Sea. Their cottage was in a row of similar buildings, which in turn were adjacent to the slipway where the local fishermen parked their boats and tractors, and which led to the long beach stretching over nine miles from the South Gare at the mouth of the River Tees all the way down to Huntcliff at Saltburn. Andrew had been born in this house shortly after his parents had married and it was a warm house filled with love. His mother had a difficult childbirth and they had decided not to risk her health by having any more children so, as a result, Andrew was the only child. He had been born with the handicap of having one leg slightly shorter than the other and because of this, as he grew older, he began to walk with a pronounced limp and had to wear a specially made platform boot to minimise the impact on his hip joints. Undeterred by this, Mr and Mrs Teach wanted him to have a normal childhood just like any other child. There were going to be no special schools for their boy and so he attended the local infant, junior and senior schools. The infant school wasn't too bad, although some of the other children could be very cruel sometimes with their taunts and name calling, which he did his best to ignore as his mother had told him, but sometimes it was hard and at times it hurt him a lot. However, it was in junior school when the real bullying started. There were three boys in the fourth year who used to go around in a gang, terrorising the vulnerable smaller kids. They were called Gary Maynard, Michael Foreman and Paul Miller. Andrew was an easy target and often the victim of vicious abuse from the three laughing older boys. They would shout things at him like, "Skip along home, cripple! You useless spastic!" and other immature cretinous phrases. Andrew both hated and feared them in similar quantities. They had not physically attacked him yet, but he knew it would just be a matter of time as he had witnessed their cowardly assaults on other unfortunate kids.

It happened one cold winter's day when school had finished and all the pupils were leaving for home, walking down the tarmac driveway that led to the main road and footpath. It had been raining and Andrew was wearing the snorkel jacket that his parents had bought for him the previous week. He had the hood up and had zipped the snorkel so that it formed like a tube in front of his face, the edging being lined with fake fur. Although this was good protection from the elements, it had the disadvantage of narrowing his field of vision. All of a sudden, someone grabbed the front of the hood from behind and closed the aperture completely; he could see nothing, and his assailant began to spin him around faster and faster to accompanying whoops of delight, which he recognised straight away. He soon lost his footing and when he was released, he went crashing to the ground, badly grazing his hands on the cold wet tarmac, his trousers soaking wet from having landed in a puddle.

As the three bullies ran off, one of them shouted, "Did you enjoy your trip, spasmo?" The cowards laughed hard at this as they disappeared into the crowd, clipping heads and punching arms along the way.

Andrew was shaking badly as he struggled to his feet, feeling both humiliated and embarrassed.

"Are you alright?" a friendly, concerned voice enquired.

Andrew looked in the direction from where the question had come. Although he did not know the boy, he had seen him around the school many times before and recognised him because of his magnificent shock of red curly hair which was a stark contrast to his own blond hair. He was a bit taller than Andrew and more stocky in build.

"I saw what they did to you, those cowards. They come after me all the time. It's because of my hair. As soon as they spot someone who is different from them then you become a target. My name's Russell Swales but my nickname's Rusty. I've no idea why." They both managed a smile at this. "I'm in the same year as you, in Mr Hall's class. Let's keep walking."

Andrew's limp was worse than ever because of the fall and his hands stung like they were on fire, but he walked on regardless.

"My name is Andrew, Andrew Teach, but you can call me Andy."

They walked together in the same direction, both of them heading for their own homes, Rusty doing most of the talking, Andy doing most of the listening, and that is how their friendship started.

Over the next weeks and months, they developed a natural rapport and soon had elevated their relationship to 'best friend' status. Both boys had been amazed at how close their houses were to each other, Rusty living in one of the many terraced houses on High Street, which was only a few hundred yards up the road from Andy's house on Cliff Drive. They soon became regular visitors to each other's homes, often taking turns at inviting each other to tea which would normally consist of something like fish fingers, fishcakes, beef burgers or sausages with home cooked chips, baked beans or peas. There was always a plate of buttered, sliced white bread with a jar of tomato ketchup and brown sauce on the table next to the salt and pepper. Afters would usually be either bananas and custard, rice pudding or Angel Delight. On an evening, they could be found playing on the beach or in the Valley Gardens and had to make sure that they were always home extra early on a school night. The reason why they had not met sooner was that Rusty's family had only moved to the area three months earlier, his father being transferred from Scunthorpe to work in the local steelworks at Redcar, which coincidentally was where Andy's dad worked as well.

The boys' versions of each other's nicknames developed over time. Rusty became Rusty Nails.

"Is that because you think I'm as hard as nails?" Rusty joked.

"No," said Andy. "It's because it rhymes with Swales, you dingbat."

They both laughed at this. Andy became Sandy because of the amount of time that he spent on the beach. Sandy was then joined with Beach because it rhymed with Teach and Sandy Beach eventually got lengthened to Sandy Beaches. So, Sandy Beaches and Rusty Nails became the new younger version of Butch Cassidy and The Sundance Kid.

"More like Hopalong Cassidy and the Sundance Kid," joked Rusty.

They were rarely apart outside of the classroom and often found themselves in all kinds of minor scrapes. They had also christened the three bullies as either The Three Stooges or The Goon Show and were constantly on their toes trying to avoid them. They in turn tagged Sandy as Clubfoot, which quickly turned into Long John Silver when the tale of his alleged ancestry began to circulate around the school, and Rusty was simply known to them as Gingernuts.

The Three Stooges were constantly on the receiving end of the headmaster's slipper because of their total lack of respect and often appalling behaviour.

Mr Metcalfe had come very close to expelling them on several occasions and very nearly succeeded after one particularly nasty event, were it not due to a lack of solid evidence.

It was the start of a school day, and the pupils were arriving at school when one of them noticed something unusual that was hanging from the branch of a tree just inside the school grounds. On closer inspection it became apparent what it actually was. Suspended by its neck on a small length of rope was a dead tabby cat, its tongue lolling out of one side of its mouth, its eyes wide open and staring with the pupils fully dilated and dried blood on its fur. It was obviously a family pet that had met a very cruel end at the hands of some sadistic bastard or bastards. The horrified children ran into the school looking for a teacher to report the apparent execution of the poor animal.

At the morning assembly, Mr Metcalfe told the school that the police had been informed and warned that if any of his pupils had been involved in what had happened then the punishment would be very severe indeed. The Three Stooges remained poker faced during his speech but over the following days when a first year student, Lee Walker, had been identified as the cat's owner, the Goon Show quickly rolled into action and began a subtle campaign of mental cruelty by doing things like walking behind him and making meowing noises or quietly reciting rhymes like 'Ding dong bell, pussy's in the well', which they thought hilarious, especially when Maynard, who appeared to be the leader of the gang, adapted the lyrics to 'Ding dong Lee, your pussy's in the tree. Who put it there? Does anybody care?'

Despite his suspicions and best efforts, neither Mr Metcalfe nor the police could find any decent evidence for them to punish the Three Stooges. Which was a shame, because his suspicions were correct, and it was them that had killed the cat and yes, it had still been alive when they had strung it up.

CHAPTER 2
1973

Sandy and Rusty were both nine-years-old and had many things in common. They enjoyed watching Top of the Pops at seven o'clock every Thursday night, their favourite bands being Slade, Wizzard and T. Rex. They were both extremely keen on collecting things like the picture cards that were included in boxes of PG Tips and Tetley Tea, and also sending off in the post for free gifts by cutting out tokens from cereal packets or sending empty crisp packets in return for various trinkets, their favourite ones being the metal WEAR-EM SCARE-EM badges that Tudor Crisps were currently offering, which depicted the images of various monsters like gargoyles or Medusa. All these things and many more were a happy distraction from the Monday to Friday slog of attending school.

One late sunny spring afternoon when the air was heavy with the scent of freshly mown grass, the boys were playing on the school field at the back of one of the prefab classrooms when Rusty spotted something jumping in the grass.

"Sandy, come and look at this," he said.

"What is it?" Sandy asked.

On closer inspection, Rusty saw that it was a tiny baby frog not much bigger than a new decimal penny. He knelt down and cupped the little creature in his hands before showing it to Sandy.

"Wow, how cool is that!" Sandy exclaimed.

They were both kneeling on the grass now and soon began finding the little fella's brothers and sisters. There was a house that had a pond in the garden at the back of the school and the small amphibians must have been involved in some kind of migration event. It was then that the bell rang, indicating the end of the afternoon playtime.

"Oh damn," said Rusty.

"Why don't we come back after school and have another look?" Sandy suggested.

"Good idea! I'll tell you what, there's some old cardboard boxes around the back of the bins, we could put them in one of those and take them home later on."

The two boys agreed on this and reluctantly trudged into the school building for the last hour of the school day, Rusty dragging his heels and Sandy limping his limp.

It was a long last hour and when the bell finally rang to end the lessons, both Rusty and Sandy headed for the 'Frog Place', hoping that they would still be there. It was Rusty that reached it first, with Sandy a few minutes behind him after he had made his way through the throng of homeward bound pupils.

"Are they still here?" Sandy asked excitedly.

"Yeah, quite a few," Rusty replied.

The two boys were on all fours again, examining the small population of even smaller animals.

"I'm gonna call this one Freddy," announced Sandy.

"I'm gonna call this one Hop Along," said Rusty, "and this one's called Freda."

"How do you know it's a girl frog?" Sandy asked.

"I can tell by the way it hops," Rusty replied, and Sandy creased up laughing.

"Okay then, I'll call this one Kiki after the frog on Hector's House," Sandy added.

They continued to name the frog family while they waited for the last of the pupils to disappear.

"I'll go and get a box," Rusty eventually said.

"Okay, I'll try and keep them together," said Sandy as Rusty rose to his feet and vanished around the side of the prefab, heading for the dustbins.

It soon became apparent to Sandy that shepherding frogs, especially these tiny creatures, was no easy task. It was actually like trying to herd cats. He picked up one at a time and tried to contain as many of them as possible in a small area of exposed earth. After five minutes, he was beginning to lose his patience as he began to experience more escapees than captures.

"Come on, Rusty," he said out loud. "The bins aren't that far away."

After a few more minutes, Sandy got two of the frogs in the palm of one of his hands and cupped the other hand on top, trapping them inside their own personal little frog prison. He decided to go and look for his friend as something didn't feel right. Rusty was a fast runner and should have been back with the box in no time at all.

Sandy rounded the corner of the prefab and walked in the direction of the bins. There was no sign of anyone. The bins were at the other side of the school building and Sandy would have to turn a corner before he reached them. As he neared the corner, he began to hear voices, some were laughing, some were talking, and one was squealing. His heart began to beat faster as he edged towards the corner of the wall where he stopped before carefully peeping around in order to see what was going on.

He quickly drew his head back and stood there frozen to the spot. It was the Three Stooges and they had Rusty. Paul Miller had one of Rusty's arms up behind his back, his other arm around Rusty's throat. Michael Foreman was taking pot shot kicks at Rusty's shins and Gary Maynard was pulling Rusty's head to one side by his hair. Rusty, in turn, was squealing with pain, his face visibly wet with tears.

"Stop squealing like a girl, you little shit," ordered Maynard, but Rusty couldn't. He thought that his arm was going to snap, and his legs were numb with the relentless kicking.

"We haven't even started yet, and why's your hair so ginger anyway? Was your mam screwed by an orangutan? Did your dad shag an orangutan?" This made Miller and Foreman burst out laughing. "Are your mam and dad having sex with orangutans?" What followed was a chorus of wild monkey noises.

Sandy was both paralysed with fear and enraged by the brutality that his friend was enduring, but he was powerless to help. What could he do? And if the Three Stooges discovered him then they would torture the life out of him, and God knows what they would do to the two baby frogs that he still had clasped in his hands. He tried to think of some positive course of action to enable Rusty to escape. Diplomacy would be useless as it was impossible to reason with psychopaths, and it would only result in his capture.

Just as he was beginning to give up hope of a solution, he caught a movement to his right. He quickly turned his head. There was a man walking from the dining hall towards the main school building, carrying a mop and a metal bucket. It was the school caretaker, Mr Hunniman, or Mr Honeymonster as some of the kids had nicknamed him, and he was slowly making his way toward them. Sandy took no chances and bravely began to advance towards Mr Hunniman but away from his friend and the Three Stooges, then he shouted at the top of his voice.

"Help, Mr Hunniman, sir, please help us. Mr Hunniman. Help!"

The caretaker stopped and looked over at Sandy who was walking towards him. It was the kid with the limp, and he had his hands clasped strangely together in front of him. Mr Hunniman placed the mop and bucket on the floor and quickly began walking towards Sandy.

"What is it?" he asked. "What's going on?"

"My friend Rusty, he needs your help. He's getting

beat up over there." Sandy pointed to the corner of the building and saw Maynard's head appear as he tried to establish what was going on. Then the boy darted back undercover as he spotted the advancing caretaker.

"Shit!" Maynard cursed.

"What's happening, Gaz?" asked Foreman.

"It's his little pufffter friend, Long John, and the Honeymonster is right behind him. Quick, we gonna have to leave Gingernuts and scarper."

Foreman released his grip and Rusty collapsed to the ground. As the bullies began to sprint towards the school gates, Maynard who was at the rear of the retreating pack, stopped and looked back over his shoulder and pointed at Rusty. "This isn't over yet for you or your crippled mate, you're both as good as dead now. You're dead, the both of ya." He then turned and tried to catch up with his two henchmen.

Mr Hunniman rounded the corner before Sandy, just in time to see the three prime suspects disappearing down the school entrance steps.

"Are you alright, son?" he asked as he crouched over Rusty, who was looking sadly the worse for wear.

"Rusty," shouted Sandy as he joined them. "Rusty, are you okay?"

Rusty raised his tear-soaked face and as he continued to sob, he managed to say, "I just wanna go home now."

It was then that they all heard a terrific bang and a loud screeching of tyres. They sharply turned their heads in the direction of the school gates and saw a council dustbin lorry which had stopped there slightly askew in the centre of the road.

At first, there were a few seconds of silence, then the doors of the lorry opened and the workers started clambering out, shouting. From the other side of the road, a woman started screaming hysterically and she was shortly joined by several more.

Mr Hunniman jumped to his feet and sprinted towards the steps and when he finally reached the pavement, the first thing he saw was Maynard, who was just standing there. He was white as a sheet, obviously in shock, and it was plain to see that he had peed in his trousers. In the road in front of the lorry, the binmen were surrounding two bodies that lay motionless, broken and bloodied. Mr Hunniman walked over and although it was difficult to tell at first with the extensive injuries, he was pretty sure that it was Maynard's two partners in crime, and they looked quite dead to him. Michael Foreman lay on his back with his right arm, which was obviously dislocated, twisted backwards and pointing upwards behind his smashed skull. Paul Miller's legs had both been broken at the knee and they were bent the opposite way to normal at ninety degrees.

Rusty and Sandy stood at the top of the steps and observed the scene before them. It was Rusty who spoke first. He had stopped crying now and, showing no emotion or sympathy, he uttered the words, "Good riddance to bad rubbish. All they have to do now is throw them in the back of the dustcart. It's a shame they never got that bastard as well though."

Rusty pointed at the pathetic figure of the trembling Maynard.

Sandy couldn't believe what he was seeing and, unable to talk, he just stood there next to Rusty with his hands still clasped in front of him.

"Come on, Sandy, we'll go the other way home. Let's get out of here."

They turned and both started limping towards the side gate in order to avoid the carnage and the chaos. They walked home together in silence to the sound of distant sirens coming from all directions.

When they reached Rusty's house, he turned to Sandy and said, "Thank you for rescuing me. You saved my life." Tears ran down his cheeks as he grabbed Sandy's shoulders and after a brief embrace, he turned, walked up the garden path and entered the front doorway.

It was then that Sandy remembered the two frogs. Throughout the whole ordeal he had kept his hands clasped and now he opened them only to reveal that the two froglets had died. He felt an intense sadness as he tipped their tiny corpses into Rusty's garden. He had let them down badly. At that moment, he heard his mam shouting as she walked quickly up the street towards him.

"Andrew, Andrew, are you alright? What are all those sirens? You're late, I thought something had happened to you." She reached him and then flung her arms around him. "I was so worried," she said.

"I'm fine, mam," he reassured her. "Honest."

"What's happened? Do you know?" she questioned.

"There was an accident."

She stopped cuddling him, held him by the arms and waited for more information.

"Two boys were run over. By a dustbin lorry." He saw the appalled shock in her eyes, and he burst out crying.

"Come on, let's get you home." She put her arm around him and led him back to their house.

Following the 'Frogs and Dustbin Lorry' incident, Mr Metcalfe finally got his chance to expel Gary Maynard from the school after Mr Hunniman's, and Sandy and Rusty's joint explanation of what they had witnessed. The headmaster had no hesitation in letting Maynard go as he was due to start the senior school after the upcoming summer holidays anyway, and he was totally unsympathetic to the boy's pleading that his dad would 'kill him' when he found out.

School life became much more tolerable for Sandy and Rusty after the departure of the Goon Show, and the next three years passed by until it was finally time to leave the junior school behind and embark on the next step of their educational career by moving up to the seniors after the six-week holidays. It had already been amazing weather for the past few weeks and the two boys eagerly awaited the long days ahead, playing on the beach. They didn't know it yet, but this summer was going to be one of the hottest ever recorded and this was the year when they were going to meet Anne Sinclair, and she was someone who was going to change their lives forever.

CHAPTER 3
THE START OF THE LONG HOT SUMMER OF 1976

Two weeks of the school holidays had already passed, the temperature so intense that the mercury was starting to explode out of thermometers, and there seemed no end in sight for the unprecedented heatwave. Sandy and his parents were sitting at the dining table, eating the Sunday dinner that his mother had cooked that morning, which was chicken and stuffing, Sandy's favourite. The conversation turned from the weather and the worsening drought situation to what their son wanted to do after he left school in five years' time.

"I quite like the idea of working in a museum," said Sandy.

His father raised his eyebrows slightly. "Sounds like an interesting idea. You're certainly good at bringing relics and souvenirs back from the beach. Mind you, you would probably have to go to college and university to do something like that. It could take years." Sandy got the distinct impression that his father was trying to put him off the idea, then he added, "You've got to remember, son, that a lot of the time it's not what you know… it's who you know. I could get you in at the steelworks, put a good word in for you. You'd be earning good money in no time." His father carried on eating and his mother, sensing a bit of tension in the room, suddenly changed the subject.

"Well, the key to happiness doesn't always have to involve money and there's plenty of water to go under the bridge before that decision has to be made."

His father nodded in agreement. "That's a fair comment."

"Anyway Andrew, me and your dad have got some news to tell you."

His father looked up with a confused and slightly shocked look on his face.

"Have we?" he asked.

"Yes, next door, you know."

His father looked relieved and smiled. "Oh yeah, you tell him, luv."

Sandy was intrigued as to what the news must be and so he listened intently to his mother.

"Well, you know Ted and Milly next door, Mr and Mrs Johnston?"

Sandy nodded his head. Ted and Milly lived to the right of their house and Mrs Bird, the old lady, who still insisted on Sandy picking a sweet out of her tin whenever she saw him, lived to the left of them.

"Well, they've never been able to have children of their own, you see, so they've been trying very hard to adopt a child to call their own. Well, a young girl is coming to live with them. They are going to be temporary foster parents but if all goes well, they will be looking to adopt her. Isn't that exciting?" she asked her son.

"Yeah, it is, mam. What's her name? Do you know?" he enquired.

"Milly told me that she is called Anne. She's the same age as you and will be going to the same school as you and Russell."

"Wow, cool. When will she be arriving?" Sandy asked.

"This Wednesday afternoon around three. I've invited the three of them to pop round for a cup of tea on Thursday."

His father cleared his throat and in a serious tone said, "You better tell him the rest, luv. He needs to know before we meet her." He gestured with his fork for her to carry on before going back to his mashed potato.

His mother sighed and her voice became softer and more solemn. "Well, it's not easy to say, so I'll just come out with it. The reason that Anne is being fostered by the Johnstons is because she hasn't got a family of her own."

"Why not?" Sandy was curious.

His mother took a deep breath and looked away, avoiding eye contact. "Well, about eight months ago there was a car crash. They're dead. It's so sad." His mother's eyes were beginning to fill with tears.

"Her mam and dad are both dead?" Sandy asked cautiously.

His mother started to cry. "You'll have to finish it off, Jim," she said, glancing apologetically at her husband.

"It's too sad." And with that, she burst out crying, put her hands to her face, rose from the table and quickly dashed up the stairs.

Sandy heard the bedroom door close. He looked at his father and swallowed hard.

His father rested his knife and fork on his plate and put his hand on Sandy's arm. He cleared his throat and started to speak. "It wasn't just her parents, son. Her two younger brothers were in the car as well. Unfortunately, they all died. The only reason why Anne wasn't hurt was because she wasn't in the car, she was playing at her friend's house at the time of the accident. I'm sorry we've had to tell you but it's best that you know in advance just so you don't raise the subject of her family when you meet her. I'm sure that she'll still be very upset by the whole sad business. It's a terrible tragedy for her. I feel so sorry for her." He rose from the table. "I'll go and check on your mam." And as he passed, he put his hand on his son's shoulder and gave it a good firm shake.

As his father climbed the stairs, a tear rolled down Sandy's cheek. He had totally lost his appetite and, as he heard the bedroom door open and close, he decided that the best course of action was for him to head for the place he knew best. He opened the front door and stepped out into the blazing hot midday sunshine. There wasn't a cloud in the sky and, as he closed the door behind him, he reflected on how strange it was that such a beautiful world could become such a sad and tragic place at the drop of a hat or the toss of a coin. He sighed and walked in the direction of the slipway that would lead him to the beach.

CHAPTER 4
THE ARRIVAL OF ANNE

On Wednesday, after he had finished eating his dinner, he headed for the front door, a ritual that was repeated every day as regular as clockwork, and his mother shouted from the kitchen.

"Don't forget that tomorrow the Johnstons and Anne are coming to see us at about eleven o'clock. You have to be here, son."

"Yes, mam, I know, but can I go out for a while tomorrow morning though as long as I'm back in time?"

"Ooh, alright, but you'd better be back here in good time," she conceded.

"I will be." He smiled at her and then he was gone.

Sandy sat on the soft sand above the high tide mark. It was the area of the beach that attracted the lighter debris from the sea, the flotsam. Things like plastic bottles, driftwood, old pieces of rope and the occasional glove or shoe would find their way into this zone, mostly deposited on a higher spring tide and left to lie as the sand would gradually dry out until the next spring tide. He hadn't wandered far from home as he wanted to be sitting discreetly on the slipway wall that afternoon so that he could get a glimpse of Anne when she arrived. He had never met the girl but already he felt an immense empathy towards her because of the sudden loss of her family. He wondered how he would feel if the same thing ever happened to him, and he decided that it was too painful to even consider. He glanced at his watch, a small Timex that his parents had got him for Christmas. It was twenty to three, so he stood up and headed for the slipway. Rusty was conspicuous by his absence because he'd gone on a family day trip with his mam and dad, which Rusty wasn't too pleased about because he really wanted to see the girl after what Sandy had told him about her.

Sandy had worked out that eight months ago would have been around Christmas time when the accident happened, which made her plight even sadder, having to revisit the memory every year, at that time, although he knew that the memory would be with her all the time for the rest of her life.

He came off the beach and reached the slipway at ten to three and picked out a good spot on the wall to sit on so that he could view his subject discreetly but be close enough to be within earshot of the Johnston's house, hopefully without being spotted. However, he was spotted immediately by his mother who was peeking out of their front bay window behind the net curtains.

"Andrew Teach," she muttered to herself, "spying on the poor girl. I don't know where you get it from." She tutted then smiled before continuing her vigil.

It was one minute to three when the car appeared, slowly driving up High Street towards Cliff Drive. It was a green Ford Cortina and it pulled up directly in front of the Johnston's house.

'Milly and Ted must be besides themselves with nerves and excitement,' thought Mrs Teach from her observation post.

The car stopped and Sandy and his mam watched as the passenger door opened and a woman stepped out. She closed it behind her and approached the Johnston's front door. Then the driver's door opened, and a man stepped out. He shut it, then proceeded to open the back door. As the woman began knocking on the front door of the house, a young girl tentatively stepped out of the car. She was dressed in a yellow tee shirt with white shorts and white plimsols. Her complexion was tanned, her hair was dark and shoulder length. She looked a couple of inches taller than Rusty and quite broad shouldered. She was pretty but her face betrayed a sadness that choked Sandy up; he thought that he was actually going to cry. He managed to hold it in and the man and girl, who was obviously Anne, joined the woman at the door. The door opened and Milly Johnston stood there with her husband behind her. She beamed the most joyful smile she could muster as she looked at Anne.

"Hello, my dear. Welcome to your new home."

Sandy thought that Mrs Johnston was about to cry at that moment and then wondered how many sleepless nights that she had endured picking the words for that first opening sentence.

"Please come inside, everyone."

And with that, they all entered the house, following Mrs Johnston. The door shut behind them and they were gone from view. The brief show was over. Mrs Teach wiped the tears from her face and went back into the kitchen, and Sandy went back to the beach, wondering how Anne must be feeling right now.

CHAPTER 5
THE MEETING ON THURSDAY

The following day at half past ten, Sandy was sitting in his house on the settee in the front room. He had already been on the beach for a while but had dutifully come home early on his mother's instruction. He had been told to go immediately upstairs to wash his hands and face and then to dress in the clean clothes that his mother had laid out for him on the top of his bed, which he had done without argument.

His father, who was working a two 'til ten shift today, was sitting in his armchair by the fireplace, reading a newspaper and smoking his pipe. He used an aromatic tobacco which was called Clan, which was actually a blend of fourteen different types of tobacco, and the smoke had a strong distinct spicy smell to it.

Sandy's mother was standing at the bay window, nervously looking in the direction of next door. She was wringing her hands slightly and kept shifting her gaze from the outside to the clock on the wall and then to the dining table which she had furnished with their best tablecloth that only came out on special occasions.

On the table, she had laid out the best china, with the teapot taking centre stage. Scattered around it were several plates of biscuits, cakes and sandwiches. "Just in case anyone is peckish," his mam had told him.

Sandy was feeling quite nervous, and you could cut the atmosphere with a knife. It was like waiting for the hangman. The time seemed to be crawling by, when his mother announced, "They're coming." She left her position at the window and stood behind the front door.

His father put the newspaper down, extinguished his pipe and then joined his wife. Sandy stood up in expectation of what was about to happen and very shortly there was a knock on the door. Sandy's mam waited a few seconds before opening it. Standing there with Mr and Mrs Johnston behind her was Anne, who was smiling a pleasant smile and wearing a white, knee-length dress which had short sleeves and was patterned with red roses.

"Hello, everyone. We'd like to introduce you all to Anne," announced Mrs Johnston.

"Hello, pet. It's so nice to meet you. I'm Mrs Teach." Sandy's mam extended her hand towards Anne who took it and they shook.

"Hello, Mrs Teach," said Anne. She sounded a bit nervous, and Sandy was sure that she would be.

"And this is Mr Teach." Sandy's dad stepped forward and in turn shook her hand.

"Hello, luv. It's really great to see you."

"Hello, Mr Teach."

"And this is our son, Andrew. Come and say hello, son." His dad beckoned him over.

Sandy joined them at the door.

"Hi, I'm Andrew." Sandy was unsure whether or not he should offer his hand. He wasn't used to these adult introductions, however a gentle prod in his back from his father persuaded him that on this occasion it would probably be a good idea. So, he put his hand out and when she held it, Sandy felt a strange sensation like goosebumps, something that he had never felt before. Her smile broadened into a grin.

"Hi, Andrew." She held his gaze and his hand for slightly longer than he thought necessary, but out of politeness he just kept shaking it and then, in an attempt to break the deadlock, he asked a question that made himself cringe.

"Do you like Dandelion and Burdock?"

Anne laughed at this and replied, "Yes, I do. I love it."

The adults in turn all joined in the laughter to Sandy's slight embarrassment but to Ted and Milly's relief.

"Well, you better come inside and have some then," his mother instructed.

As the three of them entered the Teach's household, the adults smiled and gave each other knowing looks as if to say, 'So far so good'.

"Take a seat, Anne, make yourself at home." Sandy's dad gestured towards the settee and Anne sat down where Sandy had been sitting. His dad sat back in his chair, picked up his pipe then put it down again as he was under strict instruction not to smoke 'that smelly thing' while they had guests.

Sandy perched on the other end of the settee and Mr

and Mrs Johnston sat at the dining table while his mam started fussing around like a mother hen. Firstly, she gave a glass of Dandelion and Burdock to Anne and then one to Sandy who she smiled at and winked as if to say, 'Well done, son'. She then proceeded to pour the tea as small talk broke out between the adults about the weather and the drought. The children sat in silence, not wishing to appear rude and interrupt the conversation. After a few minutes, it was Sandy's dad who turned to Anne and asked her a question.

"You won't have had the chance to go onto the beach yet, have you, luv?"

The adults went quiet as Anne replied, "No, not yet."

"Our Andrew's down there every day. I'm sure he'd like to show you around at some point, wouldn't you, son?"

Anne quickly turned her head towards Andrew and raised her eyebrows as if in expectation.

"Of course I will."

Anne's face burst into a grin of pure excitement.

"Will you really? Will you take me to the beach?"

"Yes." Sandy laughed at her enthusiasm.

She then turned quickly towards Milly who had already guessed what was coming next. "Mrs Johnston, would it be alright if me and Andrew go to the beach now?"

Sandy was impressed with her forwardness and confidence, even if it was slightly cheeky.

Mrs Johnston was unsure of what to answer as she certainly didn't want to upset either her neighbours or the young girl who she hoped to adopt one day, so she tried a compromise. "You can go to the beach this afternoon, my dear. You've got your good shoes on, see, and we've only just arrived at Mr and Mrs Teach's house."

Anne looked crestfallen.

Sandy's dad noticed this and quickly intervened to take control of the situation.

"It's fine by us, Milly, and she can take her shoes off before they get onto the sand. It'll do them good. They can get to know each other. I'm sure they don't want to sit here and listen to us old fogies boring them to death."

"Please, Mrs Johnston," Anne pleaded. "I'll take my shoes off and I won't get my clothes dirty. I won't go in the water. Please."

Milly turned to Sandy's mam. "Are you sure you don't mind, Iris?"

"Not at all. It's like Jim says, it'll do 'em good." Sandy's mam was actually hoping to have a bit more conversation with Anne, but she knew that there would be plenty of opportunities in the future.

"Well alright, go on then, but be back before twelve… and that's twelve noon, not midnight."

"Thanks, Mrs Johnston." Anne shot out of her seat and did something quite unexpected. She walked over and embraced Milly. "Thank you," Anne whispered in her ear.

All the adults were stunned into silence, Milly and Sandy's mam immediately choked up.

"You go and enjoy yourself, pet. And watch what you're doing," Milly said.

"Take good care of her, son, and stay out of mischief," Sandy's dad ordered.

"I will, dad," he replied.

"Come on then. Whatcha waiting for?" Anne then took hold of Sandy's arm and playfully pulled him to his feet. "It was nice to meet you, Mr and Mrs Teach."

"And you, luv. Take care," said Sandy's dad.

"Have fun," said Sandy's mam as they walked through the doorway closing the door behind them. The adults looked at each other and it was Milly who broke the silence.

"She hugged me. Did you see that? She hugged me," she announced before breaking down in tears. Ted, who was close to tears himself, quickly put his arm around her shoulder for he knew how much that had meant to his wife. Months of uncertainty as to how Anne would react towards them had just been blown away.

"C'mon, luv, it's alright," he reassured her.

Sandy's dad looked over and noticed that his own wife had tears coursing down her face. He stood up and joined the group at the table, putting his hand on her shoulder and because he knew that the women's tears were ones of relief and happiness and not sadness, he spoke the words. "Well folks, that seemed to go as well as it possibly could... more tea anyone?"

CHAPTER 6
ANNE INTRODUCES SANDY TO HER PAST

"What's wrong with your foot, Andrew?" Anne asked as they walked down the slipway. She had noticed his limp and the raised platform boot that he was wearing.

"It's my leg. I was born like this. The right one's a bit shorter than the other so I have to wear this special boot. It's okay but a bit of a pain when I have to take it off to paddle in the sea," he explained. "And you can call me Sandy if you like."

"Sandy?" she questioned. "Why Sandy?"

"It's my nickname. My friend Rusty gave it to me."

"Rusty? Is that his real name?" she enquired.

"No and you'll see why they call him Rusty when you meet him. He only lives up the road. His real name is Russell Swales, but I call him Rusty Nails."

She smiled at this and continued her questioning. "So why Sandy then?" She was guessing it was because of his hair colour.

"Because of the time I spend down here," he said as

he gestured towards the beach and the sea beyond it. "It started off as Andy and then Rusty changed it to Sandy and then he added Beach because it rhymes with my surname Teach and now my full nickname is Sandy Beaches."

She burst into a fit of laughter and then said to him, "Sandy Britches, I like that."

"No, it's beaches not britches," he insisted.

"Whatever you say, Sandy Britches, whatever you say." She had the cheek of the devil and Sandy just smiled and shook his head as once again she threw back her head and laughed.

They reached the end of the slipway where the paving slabs and concrete gave way to the sand so they both stopped, and Anne grabbed hold of Sandy's arm to steady herself as she started to undo the buckle on one of her shoes. Sandy immediately felt the electric goosebump feeling that he had experienced when he had first shaken her hand. It was hard to describe, but it felt exciting. She finally removed her shoes and socks and then they both continued on their walk. Sandy avoided any direct questions about Anne's background, and he kept the conversation as low key as possible, mostly talking about what he and Rusty got up to on the beach. But you could have knocked him down with a feather when out of the blue, she turned to him and asked, "Do you believe in ghosts? Because I do."

"Ghosts?!" he blurted out. "Well, I've never seen one, so I don't really know. Why? Have you?" he asked her.

"Yes," she said in a matter of fact way. "I always have done."

Sandy was amazed by this revelation and at a loss as to what to say next.

"I see them as clear as I can see you now, sometimes at night and sometimes in the day. Sometimes they talk to me and sometimes they don't."

Sandy was unnerved at the information she was sharing with him and began to worry that she might be slightly unhinged, maybe due to the shock of losing her family the way that she had. He decided to go along with what she was claiming anyway and try not to upset her.

"What do they look like, Anne?" He sounded genuinely intrigued and he supposed he was really. What if she was telling the truth after all?

She sighed then said, "Just like normal people. Some are strangers who I don't recognise but others are people who I know, love, and miss."

They both stopped walking and Anne continued to speak. "I'm sure you've been told about what happened last Christmas, Sandy, about the car accident and my family?" She was looking very serious and sad.

Sandy nodded his head and let her carry on.

"I might as well tell you the whole story." She took a deep breath and continued. "It actually happened on Christmas Eve. My mam and dad had taken my younger brothers to Woolworths to see Father Christmas and to tell him what presents they were hoping for. Phillip was seven and Billy was three. I didn't go because I've grown out of all that now, so I went to play at my friend Julie's house instead. They were on the way home when it happened." Anne looked away and swallowed hard. Her bottom lip

38

began to tremble, and her eyes filled with tears. "They came to a corner in the road, and a car came speeding around the bend on the wrong side." At this point, Anne burst out crying and looked back at Sandy. "It was a head on collision... and they didn't stand a chance... he was a drunk driver."

Sandy choked up at hearing her traumatic recollection and stepped forward and flung his arms around her. Although he couldn't speak, the warmth of his gesture mingled with the electricity between them and finally Anne calmed down. He released his grip and took a step back.

"But sometimes they come to me. They let me know that they are okay and that everything is going to work out good for me and not to worry so much about things. I always feel better when they visit me. I don't feel so alone."

Sandy felt a terrible pain of sadness for her and gently touched her hand.

"I'm glad they're okay, Anne. I'm glad for you." He was feeling incredibly sad for her but what happened next totally flummoxed him.

"In fact, they're here now." Her face had lit up with delight and Sandy let go of her hand. "Mam, Dad, Phillip and Billy." She was staring ahead of where the pair of them were standing, and then she pointed, "They're sat down just over there, see?"

Sandy quickly looked in the direction she was pointing but all he could see was sand.

"They're waving at us and smiling." She raised her

arm and enthusiastically waved back to where she had indicated.

Sandy couldn't believe what she was saying. His heart was pounding, and he had cold shivers running through his body. He was just about to ask if she was alright when she said, "Wave at them, Sandy. They're saying hello to you, and they want to meet you."

He was dumbstruck at this and actually terrified as Anne was totally convinced by what she was telling him. Once again, he just played along and reluctantly raised his hand and waved. So here he was, either waving at a family of ghosts or standing next to a deluded lunatic, neither of those options sounding very appealing to him.

"Dad says that they have seen you before. They were standing next to you as you sat on the slipway wall yesterday morning when I arrived."

How could that be, he thought, as he was sure that nobody had seen him? Was she just guessing? Had she seen him as she sat in the car? Or had they really been standing alongside him?

"Mam says that your mam was stood at the window having a good peep at what was going on too. She says that she would have been doing the same and now she's laughing about it."

That was a weird thing to say as it was impossible to see into the house because of the long net curtains. Sandy certainly hadn't noticed his mother being there and she had never mentioned it to him so he didn't know if that could be true or not.

"Come on, Sandy, don't be shy. Let's get closer and you

can say hello." She grabbed hold of his hand and as she did so, the tingle of electricity began to flow up his arm. She then took a pace forward and pulled Sandy along behind her and as they walked onwards, the most peculiar thing that had ever happened to him began to occur. At first, he thought that he must be seeing things, but he looked on in amazement as in front of him a new image began to develop. It started off as a thin mist, which began to thicken and form into solid shapes. He began to hear the laughter of children and finally the picture resolved itself. Anne and Sandy stopped walking and there, a few feet in front of them, he could see, as clear as day, a man, a woman and two boys sitting on the sand. The adults were smiling at him, and the boys were making sandcastles. He felt no fear, only wonderment, as Anne, who was still holding his hand, introduced him to her family.

"This is Andrew, everyone, but his nickname is Sandy and he's showing me around the beach."

"So, what should we call you, young man? Which do you prefer?" said Anne's dad.

Sandy was finding it difficult to believe that a ghost was talking to him and struggled to find an answer, but he finally managed to speak.

"Sandy will be fine, sir," he said politely.

"Then Sandy it shall be then, and you can call me Arthur, and this is Louise," said Anne's dad as he gestured towards his wife.

"It's very nice to meet you, Sandy, and thank you so much for looking after our Anne. We were hoping so much that she would make friends quickly and we know that you are going to be a good friend for her," said Anne's mam.

"You're welcome," replied Sandy.

"But look at the time, you two," said Anne's dad who was glancing at his wristwatch. "You'd better get a move on, it's twenty to twelve and you know you've got to be back for twelve. You don't want to be getting into bother on your first outing."

Sandy briefly wondered how he could have known this information, but he obviously did.

"Okay, dad," Anne said reluctantly.

"And be good to the Johnstons, our Anne. They're nice people and they are going to look after you well," added Mrs Sinclair.

"I will, mam," Anne assured her.

"Right, well, off you pop then. Nice to meet you, Sandy. Phillip and Billy say goodbye to your sister and Sandy."

"Bye," they both piped up, without even looking up from their sandcastles.

They all said their farewells and Anne released Sandy's hand. As the four people began to fade away, Mr and Mrs Sinclair began to wave and Sandy and Anne both returned the gesture until they had completely vanished.

Sandy turned to Anne in disbelief. "Did that really happen?" he asked.

She was still smiling and nodded her head. "Seeing is believing. So, did you see them?" she enquired.

"Yes, I did, and I heard them, I mean, I was talking with them!"

"Then you must believe it," she concluded.

"I guess so," Sandy admitted, still feeling slightly confused but full of awe and wonderment.

"Well, come on then. Let's get back home," Anne said.

Sandy noted the way that she had said home, which to him indicated that she had already made up her mind to stay with the Johnstons and that filled him with happiness. It was true that they had only just met but Sandy now knew that Anne was a really special person, and it was going to be fun having her around, and that was an understatement.

CHAPTER 7
THURSDAY AFTERNOON

That afternoon, Sandy asked his mam if she had been stood at the window yesterday when Anne was arriving. She admitted to him that she had but only out of curiosity. Then she went on to tell him that she had spied him sitting on the wall doing the same.

"Was I on my own?" he quizzed his mother.

"Well, there was nobody else with you if that's what you mean." She had a puzzled expression on her face... surely, he knew that he was on his own? "Why do you ask?"

"Oh, no reason." Sandy's dismissive answer was enough to assure her that there was a reason, but she decided not to pursue it.

"Did Anne have much to say when you were on the beach?"

Sandy knew that this was a subtle interrogation technique that his mother used to extract any juicy gossip from him.

"We talked about different things," he replied.

There was a pause before Mrs Teach asked another question. "Did she mention her family at all?"

"No, she didn't mention them." Then he added, "And neither did I." He didn't like lying but there was no way that he was going to admit to what he had seen that morning. He had a lot of thinking to do about what had happened, and that night as he lay in his bed waiting for sleep to overcome him, he thought of little else. It just didn't make sense. How was it possible for people who were dead to appear in front of you and talk to you as if they were still alive? He then remembered something that his dad had told him once when they were having a discussion about the tidal movements on the sea.

"Sometimes you can lose things, son, and they get washed out to sea but sometimes those things get washed up back to you when the tide comes in again. They end up back where they belong, sometimes by accident and sometimes for a reason," his dad had said.

Sandy wondered if Anne's family had shown themselves to him for a reason. Sandy also remembered that his dad's words of wisdom had come true a couple of weeks later when Sandy had forgotten to retrieve his bucket from the incoming tide when he had been making sandcastles. He had wandered further up the beach with just his spade and when he finally remembered about his bucket it was too late. He had gone back to the area where he had been playing and there was no sign of the bucket, which was a distinctive bright red colour with pictures of Mickey Mouse, Donald Duck and Goofy on it. The tide had advanced considerably, and the sea had claimed the bucket for itself. He was saddened by this as he had owned the bucket for a long time, and he had some very fond memories attached to it. The next morning, however, he had gone back down to the beach to look for fossils, when something distinctively red caught his eye lying on the sand about twenty feet ahead. He quickened his pace, and he couldn't believe it because there were Mickey, Donald and Goofy looking back at him from the side of the bucket. He was amazed and his dad had been right.

Sandy smiled and eventually sleep caught up with him just like the advancing tide and he was carried away by the sea of dreams.

CHAPTER 8
ANNE MEETS RUSTY

It had been arranged that the next day, on Friday, Sandy would introduce Anne to Rusty and the three of them could spend some time on the beach. At ten o'clock, Sandy left his house and went to call on Rusty first as they had agreed. As he passed the Johnston's house next door, he heard a tapping on the front window. It was Anne, smiling excitedly. She waved, then gave him a thumbs up and started making running movements as if to tell him to get his skates on. Sandy laughed back at her and gave her a thumbs up too.

"I won't be long," he shouted and set off at a quicker pace in the direction of Rusty's house.

"What's she like then?" was Rusty's first question as he closed his front door behind himself.

"You'll like her. She's cool. She's a good laugh," Sandy explained.

"Did she talk about, you know, her mam and dad and that?" Rusty asked.

"No, not at all." Once again, Sandy had decided not to

volunteer any information about the strange supernatural experience yesterday. However, he had conceded that if Anne told Rusty what had happened, then he would have to admit it and confirm the story.

They headed for Anne's house and saw her already standing at the top of the slipway. Today she was wearing a pair of denim shorts on top of what looked like a bathing costume. On her feet were a pair of plimsols and on her head was a baseball cap. She was also carrying a beach bag over her shoulder with a folded beach blanket under her arm. When they reached her, she immediately thrust out her hand towards the boy with the ginger hair, and she could now obviously see where his nickname had originated from.

"Hi, I'm Anne. You must be Rusty."

He was pleasantly surprised at her confident forthright approach, and he shook her hand. As he did this, Sandy was scrutinising his friend's face to see if there were any tell-tale signs of strange tingling feelings like the ones that he had felt. Apart from a slight raising of the eyebrows, Sandy could not detect anything.

"Hi, yeah, that's me alright. It's pretty obvious, I guess. It's nice to meet you."

"So, do you two like listening to music?" she asked them, and they both replied that they did.

"Good," she said as she reached into the shoulder bag. "Ta-da!" she exclaimed as she pulled out a portable radio, which also had a tape cassette player.

"Cool! That looks expensive," enthused Sandy.

"Oh, it is," Anne said. "The man who owned our local record shop gave it to me."

"Wow, he must have thought a lot of you to do that," Rusty stated.

"Yeah, he did," she confirmed. "He was my dad. He owned the shop and we all used to live in a flat above it."

"Nice one," Rusty said with a grin and with that, the three musketeers headed off for the beach.

The boys decided that they would head for a spot in front of the sand dunes and set up camp there for a while. On the way, Anne had told them that Mrs Johnston had packed her up with some cheese and ham sandwiches for the three of them to share and had also provided a bottle of American cream soda for them to enjoy. So, along with the radio and a rolled-up towel, the bag was actually quite a weight, and they took turns in carrying it as they hiked towards their destination.

When they arrived, Anne spread the blanket on the sand and the three of them gladly sat down on it. Sandy was in the middle with Anne on his left and Rusty on his right.

"Does anybody wanna drink?" asked Anne as she pulled the glass bottle of American cream soda out of the bag.

"Yes please," was the unanimous response.

So, she twisted off the cap and they passed the bottle between them, gulping down the fizzy vanilla tasting green liquid. It was another glorious hot summer day with the blue sky reflecting off the blue water of the flat calm sea. There was only the gentlest of warm breezes, which now and then would rustle the tall sea grass behind them in the dunes. Sandy pointed out a group of gannets that were diving head-first into the sea, obviously trying to catch the sprats which were probably being pursued by a shoal of mackerel, and Rusty pointed out three cormorants that were flying in formation only feet above the surface of the water. They looked like the Lancaster bombers from the Dambusters movie.

Anne took the radio out of the bag and placed it on the blanket in front of her.

"So, what kind of music do you guys like then?" she asked them.

"Slade are good," said Rusty.

"Showaddywaddy are one of my favourites now," added Sandy.

"Do you like Queen?" she enquired. "Because they're my favourites and they're already massive."

"I liked that Bohemian Rhapsody song but I haven't really heard much else from them," admitted Sandy.

"Well, it's time to change that," she said. "It's time to be educated. This song hasn't even been officially released yet, it's a promo copy that my dad gave me. He had quite a few contacts in the recording business, and he managed to get hold of a copy of it for me. It's called Tie Your Mother Down. Listen."

She made sure that the volume slider was up high and then she pressed play on the cassette deck. After a few seconds of crackles, there was the sound of a gong being struck and then a dirty sounding guitar began to play. The boys were staring intently at the source of the music and Anne was in turn staring intently at them, waiting for a reaction. The first minute of the song was just that slow guitar seemingly playing random chords which was eventually joined by a swirling organ, and it had no real musical cohesion. The boys were looking nonplussed, even a bit confused, and then that part of the tune stopped, and the guitarist started chugging out a proper rock riff which was soon joined by the drums and then the singer. When finally, the song kicked off for real, the reaction of the boys looked comical to Anne as they were both enthusiastically nodding their heads in time with the music.

Sandy looked around at her and gave a smile and a thumbs up, as did Rusty. Anne had already joined in with the headbanging and was even playing an imaginary guitar. The boys were both tapping their knees in accompaniment to the drumming and when the song was over, Anne stopped the tape and asked the question.

"Well, whaddaya think?"

"Cool," said Sandy.

"Rock 'n' roll," enthused Rusty.

"Yeah, I know," agreed Anne.

"So now I know what we can call you," beamed Rusty. "How about Queenie?"

"Yes, that's it," agreed Sandy. "We'll call you Queenie from now on."

"Whatever you say, Sandy Britches," retorted Anne.

"Sandy Britches!" roared Rusty, and he fell on his back, creased up with laughter while Sandy just smiled and shook his head.

"Anyone hungry?" Queenie said as she pulled the Tupperware box out of the bag.

"You bet," answered Sandy.

Rusty on the other hand was unable to answer as he was still gasping for breath after his bout of hysterics. Queenie opened the box and Sandy chose a ham sandwich while Queenie picked a cheese one. She placed the box on the blanket and turned on the radio, which was tuned to Radio One. The music of Elton John and Kiki Dee singing Don't Go Breaking My Heart blasted out from the speaker. The song had been at number one in the charts for a few weeks now and they all agreed that it was a good tune. They sat there, eating sandwiches (which had a slightly crunchy texture because of the grains of sand on their hands) and swigging the warm cream soda, with the bottle soon containing many floaters of sandwich crumbs. The songs on the radio continued and they chatted away about life in general until, after a while, Sandy announced that he was going for a short walk to see if he could find any fossils. He invited the other two to join him but they both declined, content to just bask in the sun and the heat of the day.

So off he set on his own, heading to the left in the direction of Redcar and straight towards the high tide mark and the multitude of small stones, pebbles and debris that littered the beach.

He had been beachcombing for about ten minutes in his own world of focused concentration when he decided to look back toward Rusty and Queenie and what he saw stopped him dead in his tracks. They were both still sitting down, looking the other way from Sandy towards Saltburn. Queenie had her arm around Rusty's shoulders, and they were both waving at a seemingly empty beach. Was Rusty now experiencing the same thing that Sandy had the previous day? All he could do was stare at the scene in amazement. After a short time, Queenie removed her arm from Rusty's shoulders and they both ceased waving. Sandy decided it was time to re-join the group and headed back towards them. When he reached the pair, he noticed that the radio had been turned off and Queenie was beaming a smile at him, but Rusty was looking decidedly sheepish, even shocked.

"What's up, Rusty?" he enquired, but it was Queenie who answered on his behalf.

"He's just seen them," she said. "Just like you did yesterday," she added.

So, there it was then, the cat was out of the bag, and it was now time to be honest.

"It's okay, Rusty. I have seen them. Queenie showed me just like she said," admitted Sandy. "It was her parents and her brothers." Then he paused, before adding, "And we spoke to them, and they spoke to us."

Rusty looked up at his friend with a stunned expression on his face, then he turned to Queenie.

"So, they're real then. There are such things as ghosts!" Rusty said in amazement.

"Yes," said Queenie, "and we've all seen them, so we're all equal now. We're all believers."

"And that's what we should call ourselves," suggested Sandy. "The Believers."

"Is it some sort of magic?" Rusty asked in puzzlement.

"Kind of," answered Queenie.

And, with that, Sandy sat down on the blanket and the three of them stared out to sea in silence and watched as the gannets plunged head-first into the water.

CHAPTER 9
MESSAGE IN A BOTTLE

The following morning, on Saturday, the Believers were back on the beach and the three of them stood side by side at the edge of the sea, which was flat calm apart from the few gentle waves that were struggling to gain momentum against the receding tide. In his hands, Sandy held the empty bottle of Dandelion and Burdock that he and Queenie had enjoyed drinking two days before. He had dried the bottle out and had managed to convince his mam to let him have it as he wanted to conduct a scientific experiment with it. She had reluctantly agreed and, in doing so, she waived the five pence deposit that she would have had refunded to her on returning the empty bottle to the corner shop. Earlier on, Sandy had told the other two about his idea of throwing a message in a bottle into the sea with the result of it hopefully returning to them one day. They both agreed that it would be fun, so in Sandy's front room, the three of them set about thinking of the composition of the message. Eventually it was decided to keep it very simple just in case it reached a foreign shore where the locals did not speak English, and this is what it read:

'PLEASE SEND THIS BOTTLE BACK TO US
WITH A MESSAGE IN IT.
FROM THE BELIEVERS,
SANDY, RUSTY, AND QUEENIE.
SATURDAY 14TH OF AUGUST 1976.'

Sandy had rolled up the note, placed it inside the bottle and squeezed a cork into the top of its neck. Sandy then decided to christen the glass vessel Corky Bottle. Now, standing on the beach, he passed it to Rusty because he was a better thrower. Rusty waded out barefoot into the water until he was knee deep. Queenie and Sandy looked on in excited anticipation as he gripped the bottle in his right hand and drew his arm back then pointed with his left hand at the horizon, which was blurry with the heat haze on the sea.

"God bless you and all who sail in you," laughed Rusty as he launched the projectile skywards.

"Bon voyage, Corky Bottle," shouted Queenie as she waved energetically at the flying messenger.

"God speed, Corky," shouted Sandy, who had joined in with the waving, "and bring us back some good news."

With the launch ceremony completed, they watched as Corky floated out to sea, gently bobbing up and down as it was jostled by the undercurrent. Rusty stayed in the sea in order to observe the journey of Corky as he didn't want to turn his back on the bottle and lose sight of it.

In a few minutes, Corky Bottle had totally disappeared from view and Rusty waded back to shore.

They made their way back up the beach to the soft sand where they were yesterday, all of them taking turns to carry Queenie's beach bag. Rusty's mam had provided the sandwiches today and Sandy's mam had given them each a green packet of Tudor cheese 'n' onion flavour crisps and a small plastic bottle of lemonade, which she had issued with specific instructions to bring all of the litter back home to put in the bin.

They finished eating their picnic and it was Queenie, sitting in between the boys today, who began the conversation.

"I need to talk to you both about what I showed the pair of you. I've noticed that nobody has mentioned it yet, but you need to know that we need to be open and honest with each other about it."

The boys listened intently to her as she continued.

"When you saw my parents as I was touching your hand, Sandy, and your shoulder, Rusty, did you feel the energy that I was generating through you?"

They both nodded their heads in agreement.

"Well, that is something that my mother taught me to do, just as my grandmother had taught her. Sure, you need to be born with the gift to be able to do it, but because you both have been able to witness the experience that you have had it means that you are both gifted as well. It's just you don't know it yet. So, would you like me to teach you how to do it?" she asked them.

The two boys looked at each other not quite knowing what to say.

Then Sandy looked at Queenie and spoke.

"Is it scary when you do it? And does it hurt?" he enquired earnestly.

"It's not scary, because you learn to control it, like riding a bike. And no, it doesn't hurt. I mean, did it hurt you when you saw my family?"

"No, it didn't," admitted Sandy.

"No, not at all," added Rusty. "It was just a warm tingling feeling. Quite nice actually."

"Well, there you are then, there's nothing to be scared of and when you've got used to using it, you can do amazing things with it."

"Like what?" asked Rusty.

"Well, sometimes I can hear what people are thinking and sometimes I can see things that are going to happen in the future, and they come true. That's called a premonition, and sometimes I can actually move objects without touching them, like opening doors and stuff."

"Wow, that's amazing," said Sandy.

"Can you make yourself invisible?" Rusty asked, with his eyes wide open.

"No, I haven't quite mastered that one," she said, laughing. "Here, let me show you what to do. Put your right hand out with the palm facing up."

The two boys slowly copied her.

"Then take your left hand and cup it over the top of the other one as if your about to shake some dice."

So they both did this too.

"Now you have to close your eyes, don't speak and totally relax."

The boys did as they were told and closed their eyes. Queenie kept hers open in order to observe her two apprentices.

"And now I need you to empty your mind of all thoughts and think about an experience that you have both had together in the past that has brought you closer. It might be happy or sad or even both."

The two boys concentrated and then unbeknown to each other happened upon the same event.

"Now, control your breathing, breathe in through your nose and out through your mouth. Keep your eyes tight shut until I say so and totally relax. I'm going to be quiet now for a few moments, and don't forget to breathe."

It seemed like they had been waiting for ages until Queenie finally spoke again.

"I'm going to touch you both on the forearm now," which she did, gently squeezing each of the boys' arms.

Instantly they both felt that familiar tingle of electricity, which travelled down to their hands and then into their fingers.

"Okay, you can both open your eyes now."

They did as they were told, squinting in the bright daylight as they did so.

"Now carefully lift your top hand off the other one and have a look."

Sandy went first, and the two boys gasped in amazement at what they were seeing. It was one of the froglets that they had found that day over three years ago. It was alive, blinking its eyes and gulping. Rusty did the same, and there on his palm was another froglet doing exactly the same.

"See, they've come back to you," said Queenie.

"Can we touch them?" asked Sandy.

"Go ahead and try."

Sandy reached out with a finger and went to touch the tiny animal, and when he did, his finger just passed straight through it.

"Oh my God! It's a ghost," he exclaimed.

Rusty tried the same with his and the same thing happened.

"Now watch what happens when I let go of your arms," said Queenie.

The instant she let go, the tingling sensation stopped, and both of the baby frogs slowly vanished from sight.

Over the next few weeks, the Believers enjoyed many days in the sunshine on the beach. They shared lots of adventures together but before they knew it, it was the beginning of September and time to go back to school. It was a school that none of them had attended before, it was the senior school.

CHAPTER 10
SEPTEMBER 1976.
FIRST DAY AT SENIOR SCHOOL

The first Monday morning of the new school year came around quickly enough, the weather was changing and the multitude of ladybirds that had carpeted the pavements had disappeared. Elton and Kiki were sadly no longer at the number one spot in the charts but the song would remain memorable for many decades to come. The three Believers walked to their new school together, all of them feeling rather uncomfortable, wearing their school uniforms for the first time. None of them were used to wearing shirts and ties and it was a big change from the tee shirts and shorts that they had worn for the last six weeks. Queenie opened a packet of Opal Fruits and offered them around. The boys each took one, peeled the wrapper and popped it in their mouth.

"Made to make your mouth water," stated Sandy, quoting the TV advert. "Would anyone like a Tutti Frutti?" he added as he opened the packet of sweets.

Both of his pals took a small handful and soon had the tasty treats devoured. Then it was Rusty's turn.

"Would anyone like a Fisherman's Friend?" he offered.

Sandy and Queenie both declined.

"They're gross," she said.

"My dad says they're good for your breathing."

"So, what's wrong with your breathing?" she asked.

"Nothing," replied Rusty as he put one of the lozenges into his mouth. Three seconds later, he spat it out onto the pavement coughing and spluttering. "God, that tastes disgusting," he complained as his friends burst into gales of laughter.

It was a moment that broke the tension of the anxiety that they were all feeling as they embarked on their new adventure, even though the closeness of their comradeship gave them a strong feeling of comfort and support, and it was even more comforting when they found out that they had been placed in the same class together.

Their first two days at their new school came and went without any drama and the Believers were settling in well to their new routine. However, on Wednesday morning during the break between classes when the three of them were crossing the playground together discussing the possibility of a street party next year for the Queen's silver jubilee, a voice familiar to Sandy and Rusty, but new to Queenie, called out from behind them.

"Well, well, well, who have we got here then? It's Long John Silver with his little puff friend Gingernuts, and who's this with them? If it isn't poor little orphan Annie. What happened? Did your parents abandon you because you're so ugly?" It was Gary Maynard's sneering poisonous voice, and it was full of bile and hatred. He had skipped school the last two days, playing truant, and had just returned today under the threat of his father's fist.

The three friends stopped walking and turned around to face their tormentor.

"Oh no, it's Maynard," whispered Rusty.

"Just ignore him, Queenie. He's nothing but a bully," added Sandy.

Queenie paused for a couple of seconds, observing the venomous reptile before her. He was standing there, flanked by a few of his deadbeat mates who were all smiling and laughing with glee like a pack of hyenas as, apparently, they had just found a new victim. The boys had told her previously about him and what had happened that day at junior school when they had found the frogs, so she already knew who she was dealing with. She turned towards Sandy.

"Hold this for me," she said as she handed him her rucksack of books.

He took it from her but tried to warn her off. "Just leave it, Queenie. He's not worth it."

"Don't worry," she said. "It's time to teach him a lesson." With that, she walked towards Maynard and stopped short just a couple of feet in front of him.

His self-assured grin turned into a look of puzzlement. Sandy and Rusty both noted how the playground had gone silent and everyone was now standing still and watching the unfolding scene. Queenie did not speak but as quick as a flash she shot out her left arm and grabbed him firmly by his ear, twisting it violently with all her strength as she dug her thumb into his lughole. He screamed out in pain and clutched her arm as his knees buckled underneath him. With his eyes closed, he knelt before her, his face screwed up in pain. Meanwhile his so-called pals all took a few steps backwards. None of them stepped forward to help him, shocked as they were by the fact that it was a girl that had brought him to his knees. Indeed, a couple of them had even started to walk away in the direction of the bike sheds.

"Let go of me, you crazy bitch," he pleaded.

"Open your eyes and look at me," she demanded.

He refused, so she twisted his ear even harder until it was burning like it was on fire. His eyes immediately opened but it wasn't Anne Sinclair who he was looking at. The day seemed to have turned into night and there before him was Michael Foreman and it was he who was twisting his ear with his one good arm, his right arm just hanging and swaying at his side. His face looked like he had been attacked with a hammer and whatever recognisable features had been left were contorted with rage.

"You, murdering bastard," he roared. "It was you that got us killed."

"No," screamed Maynard in absolute terror.

"Yes, if you hadn't told us to run that day then we'd still be alive. The both of us."

Maynard then noticed movement behind Foreman. On the floor, crawling out of the darkness was the deformed body of Paul Miller. He was slowly advancing towards him, his legs hopelessly broken, and he was skittering on the ground like an injured animal. But what was more alarming was the fact that his entire lower jaw was missing, as was his left eye. His right eye had completely rolled backwards just leaving a bloodshot white eyeball. He pulled himself along with his arms and was making the most shockingly disgusting primeval noises in his throat as he attempted to speak.

"We are going to haunt your nights and destroy your days from now on," growled Foreman. "Just like you have destroyed us."

"Let me go, you crazy bastard," pleaded Maynard, screaming at the top of his voice.

Queenie let go of his ear and the nightmare vision instantly disappeared from his sight. He started mumbling something about her being an evil witch, but Queenie was content that he was sobbing like a little kid, broken and humiliated, on his knees with the whole school looking on at him. She walked back to the other two Believers and took her rucksack back off Sandy.

"Thanks," she said calmly and smiled. "We won't be getting any more trouble off him."

"What did you do to him, Queenie?" asked Rusty.

"Oh, I just had a little word in his ear and reintroduced him to a couple of his old pals."

The three of them then walked off in the direction of their next lesson, leaving a stunned audience and a defeated bully behind them.

CHAPTER 11
RECURRING NIGHTMARES

From that moment on, every night, the mutilated tortured souls of Miller and Foreman would visit the petrified Maynard in his bedroom whenever he finally managed to go to sleep. The nightmares were horrendous, and the two battered corpses seemed to paralyse him with terror to the point where he couldn't even awaken himself from the torment. It was only when they had decided that enough punishment had been dealt out that he would be released back to consciousness.

When he was finally allowed to crash back into reality, slick with sweat and his heart beating out of his chest, he would just lie there and sob into his pillow until eventually it was time to get up. This had been going on for a week now and the sleep deprivation that he was suffering was having an overwhelmingly debilitating effect on every single second of his waking hours. He was beginning to look like the walking dead himself and he had a worrying feeling that he was going insane.

It was Thursday night of the following week, shortly after he had surrendered himself to the dreaded sleep which he both craved and despised, when he once again found himself delivered into the hands of his torturers and the experience took on an unexpected turn.

Foreman turned up first as usual and stood at the side of his bed with his right arm still swinging like a broken pendulum.

"You have to kill the witch," he instructed Maynard. "If you want us to leave you alone and let you get on with your life in peace then you have to kill the witch. She has put a spell on us and the only way for me and Miller to escape this eternal limbo is for you to kill the witch that did it. Tomorrow night she will be with her two apprentices at the Teach's house. Do you know where that is?"

Maynard acknowledged that he did because the year before on Bonfire Night he had followed Long John Silver home at a distance and later on in the evening pushed a lit banger through the letterbox and ran like hell.

"There will be no adults in the house, so you can kill her then and while you're at it, you might as well despatch the other two idiots at the same time. So, will you do it?"

Maynard felt that he had no choice but to agree and he nodded his head vigorously.

"Good, because if you don't, I'll set him on you." Foreman indicated toward the other side of the bed and when Maynard turned to look, he found himself face to face with the wrecked skull of Paul Miller.

His mutilated body was twitching like he was being electrocuted, and his broken legs were thrashing around on the top of the bed as if they had a mind of their own.

The guttural screams from the open orifice of his throat were splattering Maynard with stinking gobbets of blood and mucus. And when his one eye rotated back around from white to reveal a bloodshot iris and dilated pupil, Maynard sat bolt upright in bed and screamed aloud. He had been released back into reality and the pounding of his father's fist on the adjacent bedroom wall was testament to that fact. But what was reality nowadays? The edges between fact and fiction seemed to have become distinctly blurred.

CHAPTER 12
QUEEN ANNE'S REVENGE

It was Friday evening, and the three Believers' parents were having their weekly social get together at the local CIU club. On a similar note, Sandy, Rusty and Queenie also looked forward to Friday nights. After a long week of school and homework, they could finally relax and enjoy the thought of two days of freedom ahead of them. This Friday, they were all at Sandy's house. Queenie had brought her combined radio and tape cassette player, Rusty had brought the Monopoly and Sandy's mam had left them bottles of pop with sweets and crisps. They had already set the Monopoly board out on the dining table alongside the selection of goodies, which included things like Fruit Salad and Black Jack chews, and there were even some Bazooka Joe bubble gums which were always popular because of the small cartoon strip inside every wrapper.

"The radio's gone gaga so I'll have to play a cassette," announced Queenie as she turned on the tape deck and Noddy Holder started belting out the words to Cum On Feel The Noize.

The three of them sat down at the table and chose their playing pieces in anticipation of starting the game.

Gary Maynard sat at the top of the beach about five hundred yards to the right of the slipway, watching the sunset. He had made his way down here from his council house near Windy Hill Lane, following the route past St Germain's church on The Headland and descended the path to the beach in order to be hidden from his intended victims. He had brought with him a plastic Co-op carrier bag, which contained a claw hammer from his father's toolbox, a carving knife from the kitchen drawer and a bottle containing a couple of inches of Bell's whisky that he had stolen from the kitchen cupboard.

He sat there, sipping at the whisky bottle and smoking one of the three cigarettes that he had taken from his father's packet, which had been carelessly left on the kitchen table. He knew that he would have the crap beaten out of him when his father found out about the thefts, but he just didn't care anymore. The combination of lack of sleep and the nightly visitations from Miller and Foreman had pushed him to the edge of insanity. But now he had a 'Get Out of Jail' card... all he had to do was kill those three kids and his torment would stop.

The sun was now just a blood red disc, which was quickly disappearing below the horizon. The sky was ablaze with colour and Maynard knew that it would soon be dark and that was when he would make his move.

He continued his vigil and slowly drained the bottle. It had been half an hour since the sun went down and

Maynard took a final draw of his last cigarette, flicking it away, and then threw the empty bottle in the direction of the sea, which was now at high tide. He slowly rose to his feet and wobbled slightly from the effects of the alcohol, before he regained his balance. It was now time to end this madness and so, clutching his bag of weapons, he started out in the direction of his prey.

The game of Monopoly was in full flow and Rusty had actually managed to get a hotel on Mayfair just before the Go square. It was Queenie's turn to move, and she was approaching Rusty's property. She was on a Community Chest square and if she threw the two dice and scored a six then she would land on it and be liable to a very hefty fine. The atmosphere was tense as she clutched the two dice between her palms, shaking them and blowing on them for good luck.

"I want all your money, Queenie. I want it all and I want it now," Rusty informed her and then, willing for it to happen, he started chanting, "Six, six, six."

Then suddenly, Queenie stopped shaking her hands and just sat there staring into space ahead of her. Her face was expressionless, but her eyes were wide open as if in disbelief.

"What's the matter, Queenie?" asked Rusty in a concerned manner.

"I think she's having one of her funny turns. She'll snap out of it soon," said Sandy.

The boys had witnessed this before a few times and, although alarming at first, Queenie had assured them that there was nothing to worry about and it was just messages that were coming through to her.

After a short while, she did snap out of it, blinking her eyes and recoiling back into her chair. She carefully placed the dice down onto the board, the game all but forgotten.

"We're in terrible danger," she announced to the pair of them, her voice a mixture of shock and urgency. "You have to do exactly what I say. Give me your hand and you two hold hands as well."

The boys did what they were told without question.

"Close your eyes and do as I taught you, clear your minds, relax and don't forget to breathe."

After a short while, the electricity from Queenie began to flow through Sandy and Rusty, her breathing becoming deeper and heavier. It was like a television slowly coming to life and they all ended up looking at the same thing. They were outside on the beach, and it was dark. Staggering towards them was a figure clutching a carrier bag. It was like remotely viewing something from a distance through a telescope. When the figure was close enough, it became obvious who it was.

"Maynard!" exclaimed Rusty.

"Keep your eyes tight shut and concentrate," ordered Queenie, which they did without hesitation.

They watched as he removed the items from the carrier bag and let it drop to the sand.

In Maynard's left hand was a hammer and in his right was the carving knife.

"Oh my god!" Sandy shouted out. "Is he coming for us?" he asked desperately.

"Yes," replied Queenie, "but we can stop him."

"How?" Rusty begged the question of her. "We don't know what to do."

"You both have to focus harder than ever before. Trust in me and believe in yourselves that he is going to be stopped," she instructed.

"Where is he now?" asked Sandy.

"About two minutes away," Queenie informed them.

They continued to watch with their eyes closed as the desperate and terrifying image of Maynard marched drunkenly towards them. His face was contorted into a mixture of desperation and craziness, and it made their blood run cold. Then the strangest thing happened. Suddenly, the room where they were sitting filled with the strong spicy aroma of Sandy's dad's pipe smoke. It was as if Jim Teach was actually in the room with them, but that was impossible. None of them opened their eyes to check, but Sandy became overwhelmed with the urge to speak and when he did it wasn't his voice that came out of his mouth but that of his dad.

"You've got to remember, son, that a lot of the time it's not what you know, it's who you know... or who you know of."

"Who do you know, Sandy?" Queenie asked desperately. "Who do you know of that can stop him for us?" She was trying to remain calm but was beginning to sound increasingly worried.

Sandy racked his brains and was becoming desperately confused, trying to think of a solution... then it came to him.

"Of course," he blurted out to the others, in his own voice. "I know of someone who might be able to help us."

Back on the beach, Maynard staggered on. He wasn't too far away now and, although his vision had been impaired by the effect of the whisky, he still felt confident that nothing was going to stop him now from carrying out his murderous mission. It was then that he noticed something ahead of him in the sea close to the shore that hadn't been there a few moments before.

It was an old-fashioned tall ship with lanterns hanging from the masts and rigging. Travelling towards the shore from it was a much smaller rowing boat, which appeared to be full of people. He could distinctly hear the sound of the oars splashing in and out of the water and it beached on the sand in front of him in no time. He stopped walking and he could now make out a group of men disembarking onto the beach. They began to walk towards him, a few of them carrying lanterns, and he could soon make out that they were dressed as sailors, or pirates to be exact. Striding ahead in front of the group was a large man who was wearing a red coat, a tricorn hat and black leather boots. The most striking thing about him though was the big bushy black beard that adorned his weathered face. The group soon stood in front of the confused and terrified Maynard.

"Going somewhere, are we?" The man with the black beard, who must have been the captain, Maynard thought, was gesturing towards the knife and hammer. His breath stank of a thousand dead crabs like the mud in a harbour at low tide.

Maynard was dumbstruck so instead he just threw the knife to the floor and waited for the hammer to fall from his grip.

"I hear that you like playing with cats, which is good, because I have a ship's cat that is dying to make your acquaintance. The strange thing about my cat though is that it has nine tails." And with that, he bellowed out a roar of laughter which, combined with the stench of his breath, nearly caused Maynard to collapse. "Let's go and take a journey in my ship, The Queen Anne's Revenge. It'll only be a short trip, so don't you worry about getting seasick. Seize him," Blackbeard ordered his men.

Two of them stepped forward and grabbed Maynard by the arms, as another one stooped down and retrieved the two weapons from the ground.

The three Believers watched in awe as the scene played out before them. The pirates dragged Maynard to the boat and proceeded to head back to their ship.

Queenie let go of the boys' hands and the image in their heads instantly vanished like a television being turned off.

They all opened their eyes and looked at each other.

"What will they do to him?" asked Sandy.

"We might never know," Queenie replied. "But we won't be getting any more trouble off him."

"That's what you said last time," retorted Rusty, and they all just sat there in silence, staring at the Monopoly board.

CHAPTER 13
THE DISCOVERY
OF MAYNARD

It was three days later when Gary Maynard's father finally decided to report him as missing to the police. The fact that he was a regular truant from school and often didn't come home on a night were quite regular occurrences. However, over the last couple of weeks, Mr Maynard had become concerned by his son's increasingly odd behaviour. He would scream out in his sleep every single night and he had begun to behave like a zombie. His father was convinced that he had started taking hard drugs and when he noticed that his bottle of whisky had been stolen and the fact that he hadn't turned up for three days, he knew it was time to involve the authorities.

It was two days after he had been reported missing that the naked body of a teenage boy was discovered washed up on Skinningrove beach, a few miles south of Marske. It was quite badly decayed but was eventually identified as being Gary Maynard. The most startling thing though was the amount of deep cut marks on his back, his buttocks, and the back of his legs.

The toxicology report found that he had a large amount of alcohol in his bloodstream, and it was finally concluded by the forensic investigators that Maynard must have got drunk and decided to go skinny dipping in the sea. His injuries were consistent with being struck by the propeller of a fishing vessel or other type of boat and the final cause of death had been drowning.

The coroner recorded a verdict of misadventure.

CHAPTER 14
PRESENT DAY

Andrew Teach, or Sandy Beaches, was still looking for fossils on the beach as he concluded his trip down memory lane. It all seemed like a lifetime ago now and he supposed that it was really, even though he could remember it better than some things that had happened yesterday.

Unfortunately, Queenie and her adoptive family had moved away to Cornwall just a few months after the Blackbeard incident. She had kissed him properly for the first time in his life and told him that she loved him before she left, which gave him his first broken heart from which he still hadn't fully recovered. She also handed him a box, a small antique treasure chest which measured about twelve inches by eight. It was made of weathered oak which had taken a battering over the years but the black leaded iron straps and clasps that held it together were in amazingly good condition.

"This is a family heirloom and the only thing of any real value that I have," she said. "My mother gave it to me shortly before she died, but I want you to take it as something to remember me by."

It had been a few weeks before the accident on Christmas Eve and Anne's dad, Arthur, had been getting the Christmas decorations out of the loft.

"Look what I've found," he said as he passed the antique jewellery box down to Anne's mam, Louise.

"Oh my! I haven't seen that for years," said Louise as she took the box from him. "I seem to remember that we put it up there out of the way. I didn't care for it much. I think it was due to the fact that my mother gave it to me shortly before she had the heart attack."

Arthur looked down from the hatch in the ceiling and noticed the sad look on his wife's face.

"Would you like me to put it back?" he asked.

"No," she said after a short pause. "I have an idea. Anne's old enough now, I think the time's right."

On Christmas Eve, during the daytime after they had eaten their dinner and before the trip to see Father Christmas, Louise and Arthur called her and her two brothers into the front room where the festively decorated tree was.

"Okay, we know you're all excited about getting your presents from Father Christmas in the morning, so just to tide you over until then me and your dad have decided that you can open one present each from us right now."

The two boys jumped up and down and whooped with joy, and Anne beamed with glee and clapped her hands together in excitement. Arthur handed the boys their presents and they instantly began tearing at the wrapping

79

paper. Louise gave Anne hers and she sat down with the present and began to remove the wrappings which revealed an old antique treasure chest.

"It's a family heirloom," explained her mother. "It's a jewellery box that has been passed down through the generations. My mam gave it to me shortly before she passed away but now I'd like you to have it so that one day you can pass it on too."

"It's beautiful. Thank you," said Anne as she tried to open the lid, which refused to do so.

"Apparently no one has ever managed to open it, I know I never could."

Anne looked closer and noticed all of the marks on the box where obviously many people over the years must have tried to prise it open. "There is a story that goes with it though which is why you should always keep it safe."

"What's the story?" Anne asked her mother.

"That'll have to wait for another time, my dear. We have to get going, time's moving on, you have to go to Julie's house, and we have to go to Woolies"

Anne nodded her head and looked down at the jewellery box that she held on her knee. She was sensitive to many strange things and the sensation that she was getting from the box was not a very pleasant one.

•

Sandy took the box and was overwhelmed by the amount of trust she had put in him, not to mention the hint of a reunion in the future, which filled him with welcome hope. Holding the box made him feel totally happy and warm.

"I need to quickly tell you about the box. You see in all honesty it has always given me a bad feeling, especially with what happened to my family. It feels cold to me as if it doesn't want me to have it."

"That's strange," said Sandy. "Because it makes me feel totally the opposite."

"Apparently there is a story that goes with it, but… I never got to hear it," Queenie told him mournfully. "I think it might be cursed so be careful. Keep it safe."

"Why would you give me a cursed box?" asked Sandy.

"Because ever since I moved here, I got the distinct impression that it belongs to you. I think that it belongs in your family and not mine." Queenie explained.

"Any particular reason?"

"Like I said, I don't know the story and the box won't tell me… if you know what I mean, and with you I don't think it will be a bad curse, more of a blessing. If we knew the legend then we'd know the truth, but in the future, who knows… one day we might." She shrugged her shoulders. "But for now I have to go, time moves on."

She kissed him on the cheek and turned and walked away. Sandy always regretted that at that point he never had the courage to say, "*I love you too.*" And as the car drove off it was too late anyway.

He also had to say goodbye to Rusty not long after when his father was transferred to the steel works at Port Talbot. It was a really sad time, and Sandy still missed them to this day. They wrote a few letters to each other at first but that exercise soon fizzled out as real life took over.

Things had changed a lot over the years. Both his mam and dad had sadly passed away, which had left a massive hole in his life, and different neighbours had come and gone. He seemed to have spent a lot of time trying to tie up loose ends but sometimes the knots never tied, and so they remained loose forever, just flapping around like a ripped flag flogged by the weather on the top of a ship's mast. He was still living in the house that he had grown up in and was working part time nowadays at the small local museum, which was called 'Winkies Castle' and, although he got to meet people through his work, he still felt all alone in the world most of the time.

It was then that something caught his eye up ahead, poking out of the beach. As he approached, he could see that it was a fizzy drinks bottle with a cork in it. He reached out and pulled it from its position in the sand.

"Oh my god, I don't believe it," he said in astonishment. "Corky Bottle, you've come back to me."

He took a deep breath and carefully removed the cork, which was the same one that he had placed in there years ago. Inside was what looked like some kind of plastic wrapping. He managed to coax it out of the bottle and realised that it was a Clan tobacco pouch, the same kind that his dad used to smoke. He opened it up and the spicy odour immediately brought back a thousand memories. To his amazement there was a note inside.

Tentatively, he removed the piece of paper from the baccy pouch, unfolded it and read the contents:

'Life has always been a puzzling question to you,
but now you have found the answer'

"I'm more puzzled now than ever," he remarked out loud to the empty beach. The message was unsigned and undated but that didn't matter, he was just amazed that the bottle had come back to him again after all this time, however the riddle that it contained was quite bemusing.

He put the note in his pocket and placed Corky Bottle into the shopping trolley and was about to turn and head for home when he noticed something else partially buried in the sand.

It was another bottle.

He walked up to it and picked it up. It was a Bell's whisky bottle. He unscrewed the top and was amazed to see another note inside.

He managed to retrieve it and then his blood ran cold as he read it:

'IT'S OVER FOR YOU, LONG JOHN
YOU'RE GOING TO DIE
I'M COMING TO GET YOU
SO START BELIEVING THAT.
SEE YOU SOON'

Sometimes things come back to haunt you for good or bad. Some things never leave you and you just have to learn to live with it, but this was one loose end that needed to be tied up for ever.

Sandy was in no doubt as to who had written the

second note and as he stared out to sea at the horizon, he had no idea of how he was finally going to bury those particular ghosts.

God, how he missed his friends.

PART 2
THE SPECTRUM

PROLOGUE

It takes many different kinds of elements to make up the whole and there has to be a lot of small cogs to enable the big wheel to turn. There are a lot of stories that go towards making up a single lifetime and a multitude of lives are involved in creating the complete story. We each belong to a bigger picture, and we are all individual pieces in the universal jigsaw. We are completely different parts who are terminally related by the common denominator of birth and life and, in the course of our journey through this tangible Earthly existence, not everything is as it seems.

We may stare up at the night sky and observe the stars above us, but the fact is that the suns and planets that we are looking at are not actually in that position in the sky due to the time that it takes for the light to travel to Earth. What we are seeing is something that has happened in the past. For example, a star that is ten million light years away from us will be observed in the position it was in ten million years ago, and not where it is now. Even pure white light itself is essentially not pure but made up of a spectrum of other different colours with totally different wavelengths.

Now and again, we are privileged to witness the

phenomenon of a natural rainbow in the sky, even if it is just for a short period, and just as the rainbow fades away so eventually must all of us.

After our mortal refraction during our time on Earth is finished, we all end up returning to where we came from to be united again in the one pure white light. Or do we spend eternity flying through the universe at the speed of light? Or are we all destined to be captured by a black hole where even light itself cannot escape, only to be transported by an irresistible vacuum into a parallel universe of no return?

Everyone has a ghost, or ghosts, haunting them. Some are just skeletons in closets and others are just memories of the past. Some are real and some are just dreams, or a trick of the imagination, but one day we will all be ghosts in other people's lives, maybe people who haven't even been born yet. Who will you be visiting or haunting in the future, maybe in a hundred years' time, or maybe as early as tomorrow?

CHAPTER 1
RED

Richard Redman was on the run again. It seemed that he had been running all of his life, and he guessed that he probably always would be until the end of his time on Earth. He wasn't trying to evade being caught by the law, and he wasn't trying to run away from any debt collectors, he was just trying to run away from himself. He was his own worst critic and his own worst enemy. Over the years, he had discovered that he had an uncanny ability to destroy every good thing that he had either created or built or whatever he was invited to become a part of.

Tonight it was New Year's Eve and he found himself in a small bar in the gothic quarter of Barcelona that he had stumbled upon after walking down a side street just off the busy main road of Las Ramblas which eventually leads to the Christopher Columbus statue and the harbour beyond. He was sitting inside by himself at a table, drinking a glass of Beaujolais Nouveau while enjoying old 80s music, listening to Simply Red singing Holding Back the Years as he people-watched the crowds thronging through the narrow street outside. It was New

Year's Eve and he had promised himself to paint the town red tonight. There were a lot of families on the streets even though it was dark and cold, and he smiled when he spotted a red nosed clown walking past the window holding a bunch of floating balloons, offering them to children and their parents.

On the other side of the narrow street, a couple were sitting outside, underneath a heater, being hassled by an old gypsy woman with white hair and a face that was wrinkled beyond belief, who was attempting to sell them a single red rose. Richard thought she looked like the witch from the Disney film Snow White. The music changed to a song by Nena, who started singing about ninety-nine red balloons that were apparently floating by.

Richard drained his wine glass and decided to look for pastures new. He fancied listening to some live music and so he set off to see if he could discover a venue that was offering that kind of entertainment tonight.

It wasn't long before he found somewhere. The unmistakeable sounds of a live rock band playing Little Red Rooster by The Rolling Stones was permeating from a nearby bar.

However, before he approached the establishment, something made him look up. Directly above the bar, three floors up, was a woman standing on a Juliet balcony, and she was smiling at him. She looked like Vivien Leigh, who had played Scarlett O'Hara in the film Gone With The Wind, the only difference being that this woman was a redhead and the red light behind her only served to enhance her hair colour. She winked at him, blew him a kiss, and then pointed to a door at the side of the music bar.

"Why don't you come up and play with me?" she teased him, still smiling and beckoning with her finger. "I won't bite you. I'll even let you be the Big Bad Wolf if you want to be."

He smiled back at her and then thought, why the hell not? He was a red-blooded male after all and he wasn't in any kind of relationship at the moment and it was New Year's Eve, for God's sake. He pointed at the door, and she nodded.

"Come on in," she invited, and so he did.

After half an hour, he left her room, descended the red carpeted stairs, and exited the building to the strains of the band next door who were now playing Ruby Tuesday. He was feeling pleased with himself, as he appreciated simple business transactions like that, no red tape and everyone's happy. He re-joined the masses who had descended on Las Ramblas and began to make his way down the hill, noticing that behind him at the top of the road the Spanish police had already barricaded the entrance off with various vehicles and barriers as it was obviously going to be a very busy night.

As he made his way down the street, jostling with the crowd, he passed through an area of market stalls. There was a lot of artwork and jewellery on display, but he wasn't tempted to stop and buy anything as that would be a cardinal sin, a total waste of euros that, tonight of all nights, were reserved for revelry and ruin. He passed by a busker who was singing a song by Pink, and she actually sounded quite good, but he didn't stop. He headed up another narrow lane off the main street to find some more quirky bars, and it wasn't long before he found himself seated inside one, drinking a delicious glass of Burgundy. They seemed to like their progressive rock music in here as he had already been treated to songs by Genesis, Marillion, Pink Floyd and now King Crimson. Outside was becoming busier and he was on red alert to guard against the notorious army of pickpockets who worked this city.

When he had finished his drink, he made the decision to go and get some fast-food from somewhere as this would probably turn out to be a long night, so he left the bar and went in search of some sustenance. It wasn't long before he was standing in front of a burger stand. He ordered a large hot dog, adorned with caramelised red onions and a generous covering of tomato ketchup. As he stood at the side of the stall devouring his meal, he couldn't help but notice how many Chinese tourists were present tonight and he had also frequently heard the brusque accent of Russian voices everywhere he had been. This place was obviously an attraction to the Communist elements of the world for some reason. Maybe they were plotting a takeover, he mused to himself, in order to get the red flag flying here which would probably not be a good idea with Spain's reputation for bullfighting. That could lead to all sorts of complications, he thought, and he laughed to himself as he finished off the hotdog.

As he prepared to move on from the fast-food stall, a commotion broke out right in front of him. A man was wrestling with a girl who was screaming and shouting in Spanish. They were soon joined by two policemen, who restrained the girl. He guessed that she must be an active member of the pickpocket brigade and she had just been caught red-handed.

He moved on and as he passed by a narrow passageway the old gypsy woman with the white hair appeared from it and blocked his way. She offered him the single red rose that she held.

"One euro, señor," she said.

In order to avoid an argument, he gave the woman a one euro coin and she gave him the rose, then she abruptly just vanished into thin air. Richard couldn't believe his eyes. He spun around but she was nowhere to be seen. Was she some kind of bizarre street performer?

Richard decided to quickly continue on his journey towards the harbour area and as he did, he looked at the rose that he was holding and to his astonishment it was dead and wilted, its brown petals already falling off. He immediately threw it to the floor and was unable to comprehend what had just happened.

On his way, he visited several other bars, ending up at the bottom of Las Ramblas shortly before twelve o'clock. He had been informed earlier that there was going to be a huge firework display at midnight which interested him greatly as his last job had been as the owner and stage manager of a pyrotechnics company back in the UK. Unfortunately, he had run into major financial difficulties after several institutions had refused to pay fully for the events that he had organised, stating that they were under par and not what they had been promised. Very soon he had moved out of the black and into the red, suffering more red-letter days than he could stand. He eventually decided to close the business and nowadays just managed to make a living out of doing any job that he could find.

His mobile phone vibrated in his trouser pocket, so he stopped and took it out. There was a new email, he touched the screen and opened it. It was a message from a firm of solicitors back in the UK.

Dear Mr Redman,

You are cordially invited to attend the reading of the last will and testament of the late Ms Josie White at our office in Lydd, Kent. We feel that this would be in your best interests and on your acceptance, we will forward the appropriate details of time and location onto you.

Yours faithfully
White, Grey, Black & Co. Solicitors

He was jolted out of his thoughts when the explosions started overhead. Multicoloured flashes and sparks filled the sky to the delight of the gathered crowd as the firework display heralded the dawn of a New Year. What Richard didn't know at this point in time, however, was that the events over the coming months were going to change the direction of his life forever.

CHAPTER 2
ORANGE

"Of course, I won't be long. By the way, do you want to hear a joke?" said Charlie Clementine as he spoke into his mobile phone. "What's orange and sounds like a parrot?"

"I don't bloody know," replied Max Normandale.

"A carrot, of course, you thick sod." Charlie laughed out loud.

"Haha very funny, you bloody clown. Look, just get your arse down here pronto, I'm losing customers."

"Relax, bro, I'm on my way. I'll be about five minutes. Ciao ciao, Mickey Mouse." And with that, he hung up.

Charlie Clementine was a self-employed maintenance engineer, or a jack of all trades if you prefer, and he lived and worked in Scarborough in North Yorkshire. He specialised, however, in the upkeep and maintenance of the many fairground attractions, amusements and rides that the town was well known for. It was these attractions, as well as everything else that the seaside resort had to offer, which had provided a magnet for holiday makers and day trippers for years, and today was no exception. It was the start of the tourist season, and it was the bank holiday Easter weekend, Good Friday to be exact at the beginning of April. He had managed to find a place to park his white van on Valley Road at the South Bay, which hadn't been easy as the town was already starting to fill up with traffic, even though it was just past mid-morning, which was probably due to the unseasonably warm weather. He was walking along the Foreshore Road in the direction of the harbour, carrying one of his metal toolboxes, in response to an urgent callout from his friend and best drinking buddy, Max.

Charlie felt the toolbox becoming heavier the further he walked, so he swapped it from one hand to the other and thought that by the time he reached his destination he would have arms like an orangutan. He still had a fairly long way to travel as Max's ride was all the way to the end of the entertainment strip on the seafront. It was a really lucrative business during the holiday season and this morning it had suddenly broken down for no apparent reason. The ride was the only one of its kind in town and was very popular with people who wanted to scare themselves to death in order to feel alive.

Charlie had already passed the Grand Hotel, the Olympia Leisure complex and the huge Ferris Wheel that had been situated on the site of the now demolished Futurist Theatre. He had recalled going to see many famous acts there over the years, including the spiritualist medium Derek Acorah, who was a TV celebrity, and in October of the year 2000 Charlie went to see him. He was well known for his appearances on the ghost hunting series Most Haunted and it was a one-man stage show whereby

Derek would attempt to connect some members of the audience with their dear departed loved ones. Charlie had been very impressed with him and, although he hadn't been singled out for a reading himself, he thought that Derek was either a very talented illusionist/magician or that he was actually speaking to dead people. Charlie passed the Coney Island amusements with its Zoltar fortune-telling machine, which was just like the one in the film Big, which starred Tom Hanks, and then he walked by Gilly's Leisure Centre. Next there were a number of souvenir shops, and then the Terror Tower, which was an automated waxwork walkthrough of various horror film sets. Charlie had been called out here many times, mainly because of the malfunctioning of the Alien and Predator monster mannequins, which were extremely unsettling to work on as they were so lifelike and he had to try very hard to focus on the job in hand with the electronics and not be drawn into staring at the terrifying creatures, which had the unnerving look of being capable of bursting into life at any second and mercilessly ripping him to pieces. He passed by the Pacitto's and Jaconelli's ice cream shops and inhaled deeply when walking past The Fish Pan whose aroma of freshly frying fish 'n' chips was so intoxicating that it almost caused him to salivate. He ploughed on through the thickening crowds and passed many more eating, drinking and entertainment establishments, including The Harbour Bar, which was well known for serving Knickerbocker Glories, and Winking Willy's, which was another chippy. There were a few pubs down here, The Lord Nelson, The Newcastle

Packet, and The Golden Ball, which were all regular haunts of theirs. He glanced to his right and looked at the whitewashed lighthouse at the harbour entrance with the statue of the Diving Belle which stood directly in front of it. She was posed majestically in the permanent position of a crucifix with her arms outstretched at her sides waiting for the moment when she would plunge in a swallow dive into the cold North Sea, a movement that sadly she would never actually get the chance to execute.

The smell of deep-fried doughnuts and waffles from the fast-food stalls filled his nostrils and, after a few more minutes, he finally reached the ghost train where Max was pacing up and down outside, talking into his phone and holding a can of Tango in his other hand with his Great Dane dog, who was called Scoob, loyally sitting not far away.

"You took your time," he scolded Charlie.

"I'm bloody knackered, mate," was Charlie's response.

"Well, that makes two of us then. If you can't get her up and running, I'm going to lose a bloody fortune."

"What's the problem?"

"Well, I was hoping that you could tell me that," Max added sarcastically. "The whole thing just died on me. I was giving her the first trial run of the day and the power just went off, the lights and everything."

"Don't worry, bro, the future's bright. I'll have a look at it and see what we can do."

Charlie entered the control booth and, being familiar with the setup, he immediately turned the master electrical isolator to the off position, which gave him the confidence to start examining the other components of the circuit and hopefully troubleshoot the problem. All the fuses were intact, and after a few minutes, Charlie began to scratch his head.

"Well, whaddaya think?" asked Max.

"I don't know. There's nothing obvious here. I'm going to have to go in and walk the line. I might have to reset a circuit breaker or something."

"Rather you than me, pal. Watch out the Bogeyman don't getcha." And with that, Max laughed a mocking laugh that only true friends could really appreciate.

Charlie took a torch out of his toolbox and turned it on. He then picked up his tools and pushed the first of the double doors open before entering the foreboding tunnel which was the beginning of the ghost train ride. He carefully edged his way forward and began meticulously checking for any signs of damage. He was particularly looking out for blown lightbulbs, severed cables or if any of the circuit breakers on the track had been tripped out. All the time that he was doing this, he was very conscious of the grotesque figures who were observing his progress. He had a threatening audience of skeletons, werewolves, vampires, ghouls, demons, and mutilated corpses for company but, being the professional that he was, he just tried to focus on the job in hand. He made his way through various double doors and sections of the ride until he came to the base of an incline, and that is when he first saw the flicker of a light on the ceiling at the top of the rise. Maybe this was the source of the problem, he told himself, although the light seemed to be moving from ceiling to wall and was not coming from any visible source, and why was there any light here anyway for he had personally isolated all the electrics in the control booth? Then he nearly jumped out of his skin when the unseen door on the other side of the hillock slammed shut. What followed was the distinct noise of somebody walking up the other side of the track and then the groaning started, like somebody was in pain.

"Is anybody there?" Charlie enquired.

The light became more intense, reflecting on the ceiling, and it was then that his torch went out. He looked down at it and shook it violently but to no avail and when he looked up again, he saw, standing at the peak of the incline, a figure which had the terrifying head of a werewolf which was being illuminated by a torch that it was holding. The creature raised its head backwards and uttered the most horrific blood curdling howl. Charlie fell backwards and landed in the arms of a skeleton that was sat by the side of the wall. The beast began to advance down the tracks towards him but then in a surreal twist to the situation, it started singing.

"Oh, my darling, oh my darling, oh my darling Clementine. You are lost and gone forever, oh my darling Clementine. He was a miner 49'er…" Then the creature burst out into uncontrollable laughter. It stopped walking and bizarrely pulled its own face off.

"Gotcha, Charlie boy!" Max waved the mask with a grin. "Sorry, mate, but I just couldn't resist it."

"You bloody idiot," Charlie shouted at him, even though he was relieved that it was Max and not the beast from hell that he had originally thought. "You nearly gave me a heart attack. And why are you clowning around when I'm trying to fix the damn thing for you?"

"Sorry again, mate, but like I said I just couldn't resist it, especially as it's the tenth anniversary of what happened."

"Well, whatever happened back then I'm actually glad that you've turned up now because my torch has gone out. Here, give me yours and we'll check the line as we walk out together."

Max passed his torch to Charlie who had decided not to enquire about what had happened ten years ago as it was probably some sob story concerning one of Max's many failed relationships and he could do without the earache. They started walking up the track but then they both paused when they heard the door on the other side of the bank creak open and then slam shut. They stood still frozen in terror and they both distinctly heard the sound of footsteps slowly traversing up the other side of the incline.

"There's nobody else in here," whispered Max. "I locked the front doors before I came in the tunnel."

The footsteps steadily approached the brow of the hill and then like a scene from a horror movie two shining green eyes appeared over the ridge. Charlie quickly swung the torch in the direction of the demonic eyeballs, only to reveal Scoob, Max's Great Dane. He was standing there, looking innocently perplexed, and the two men just simultaneously burst out laughing. It was then that the ghost train's siren screamed its terrifying wail, and the strobe lights began flashing. The howls and screams from the audio system began and various robotic mannequins sprang into action. It was obvious that somehow the electrics had been reinstated, and Frankenstein's monster started to move with a new lease of life.

"It's impossible," stated Charlie in a tone of panic. "I switched off the main isolator, there's no power, and you've locked the doors, there's no one else in the building. Tell me that this isn't another of your stupid pranks."

That's when they both heard one of the cars shunt itself forward and move through the first set of double doors to begin its journey along the track towards them.

"Oh shit!" exclaimed Max. "No, mate, this is no joke and we've got to get out of here quick."

There wasn't much room between the tracks and the side walls, and they both knew that a collision with the car was a definite probability, so without prompting, they both began to scramble up the incline in order to vacate the tunnel. Scoob had already used his initiative and exited the ride as the two men stumbled across the railway sleepers and through the sets of doors. The car had gathered speed and was crashing through double doors behind them as it relentlessly closed the gap on the terrified fleeing duo. Max knew that they were nearly out but heard the car rattling down the incline at speed. It crashed through the doors at the bottom and was now too close for comfort, so Max grabbed Charlie and forced them both into a shallow recess in the wall of the tunnel where he was confident that they would be safe from the passing vehicle. They could hear that the car had now slowed down considerably and, as it nudged its way slowly through the doors directly behind them, the siren sounded, and the strobe lights began flashing again. They began watching as it emerged through the doors, and they were both amazed to see a young teenage boy sitting in the car.

"Oh, I get it now. You've paid one of the lads off the seafood stalls to help you to wind me up. Nice one, you nearly had me there for a minute, you clown," said Charlie.

The young boy stared at them both with a penetrating look of pure evil and, as the car passed, he never blinked, he just turned his head accordingly in order to keep his gaze fixed upon them. As the car moved forward, the boy's head just kept on turning until it had grotesquely rotated one hundred and eighty degrees and as it exited out of the ride through the last set of doors, the men were left with the eternal nightmare image of a boy with his head on back to front, staring mercilessly at them both. The doors slammed shut, they heard the car come to a standstill and the power went off again.

"What in the name of Jesus Christ of Nazareth was that?" Charlie blurted out. He didn't need to see Max's shocked and terrified expression to realise that this was no wind up.

Max was freaking out and the air was blue with obscenities and although they were both intimidated by the thought of confronting the thing again, they instinctively knew that they had to leave the tunnel, and fast. Cautiously, they opened the doors and peered into the daylight of the entrance parlour to the ride. There was nobody else there apart from Scoob, who was cowering in a corner, whimpering. The two men emerged and then, after Max had checked that the glass doors were still locked, he began to speak.

"I've got something I have to show you," he said, his voice faltering and weak.

"Are you alright?" Charlie asked as Max grabbed him by the elbow and led him to the control booth. They both entered and, as Charlie glanced at the master isolation switch that was still in the off position, Max reached under a shelf and pulled out an old well-read paperback book.

•

The ghost train had been closed down ten years earlier on this exact date because of what had happened. A fifteen-year-old boy called Martin Black, and his three mates, had been drinking illegally purchased Woodpecker cider and Oranjeboom lager at the foot of the castle that was perched on the headland between the North and South bays. They had made their way in a stupefied manner, laughing and joking, down to the 'Bottom End' of town and the amusement arcades. They stopped at the ghost train and decided that it would be a damn good laugh to have a go on it. Martin and another one of his pals got into the first car and the other two jumped in the one behind. Having paid the entrance fee, the first car moved forward to the sound of a screaming siren which mimicked the Jericho sirens of the World War Two Luftwaffe Stuka dive bombers. Strobe lights had been activated as the car nudged its way through the first set of double doors. Inside it was dark, the only illumination coming from the lighting that was directed onto the mannequins.

"BOO," shouted Martin as he grabbed his friend's shoulder.

"Get off, you bloody idiot," he shouted back.

Martin was already in stitches laughing when all the lights went off and the car suddenly stopped. The car jolted forward then came to a halt once more. Martin had stopped laughing and was now clutching onto the safety bar in front of him. All was quiet… then the lights suddenly came on. A witch's face was only a few inches away from his. A terrifying loud cackling scream pierced the air then they were plunged into darkness again and the car moved forward once more. Martin ducked down as he feared his head would collide with the witch who had the uncanny resemblance of the one out of that Disney film with googly eyes and a crooked nose. The lights came back on and it was his friends' turn to laugh at him.

"What you doing down there? You're not scared, are you?"

Martin quickly sat upright. "No, of course I'm not. You're the only pussy on this ride." And then followed up with, "RAAARGH," straight into his pal's ear, his hands posed liked claws. They both started laughing but stopped at the sound of a howling wolf beyond the next set of doors. The car pushed through them and headed around a sharp corner where the noise was coming from. Once again, the lights went out and the car juddered to a halt. Silence was quickly followed by a blood curdling howl and then the nearby guttural growling of some unseen beast. Neither of them spoke then the lights went on but there was nothing there.

Martin turned to his friend who had his eyes tightly shut. He laughed. Then the lights went out again and Martin stopped laughing. The howling of the beast returned and the lights flashed on, and there before them stood a terrifying werewolf, its eyes glowing red, its jaws opening and shutting to reveal huge incisors. They both screamed but after a few seconds the automaton was hauled back up to its hiding position in the ceiling and the car moved on.

When they were over three quarters of the way through, the car slowly approached the bottom of a short but steep incline, and it was here that Martin spontaneously jumped out of it.

"What the hell are you doing?" shouted his friend, half laughing, and half concerned.

"Don't worry. I'm going to scare the shit out of the others when they come through," Martin replied, as the car ascended and disappeared over the summit. He scrambled up the track, planning to jump out on his unsuspecting victims at the base on the other side of the drop. He waited in position in the darkness, pumped up with Dutch courage and it wasn't long before he heard the second car climbing up the hill. It reached the peak and started to plunge towards him. But he'd totally misjudged the speed of the vehicle. In the confusion of the noise and the darkness, the speeding car hit him square on. He was catapulted through the air, somersaulting like a rag doll. When he landed back on the tracks, it was head-first, and his neck was instantly broken. What followed next was an hour of total chaos and, unfortunately, despite the best efforts of the paramedics, Martin Black was pronounced dead at the scene.

The local council instantly closed the ghost train down and it was a full two years after the inquiry had concluded before it was allowed to open again due to the fact that the management of the attraction were not to blame for what had happened and it was just a tragic accident caused by the victim's own careless acts. During those two years, the owner of the ride had suffered from chronic depression and, although the verdict was favourable towards him, he had already decided to sell the ghost train as a going concern. That is when Max Normandale had stepped in and, spotting the potential of owning a ghost train that could really be haunted, he had bought it up immediately.

•

Back in the control booth, Max opened the book and removed a piece of folded paper from within its pages. He smoothed it out on top of the shelf and Charlie noticed that it was an old newspaper cutting. The headline read 'Local Boy Killed in Ghost Train Accident' which triggered something in Charlie's memory, and below that was a grainy black and white photograph. Max pointed at the picture and Charlie bent down for a closer inspection of the image. There was no doubt about it, the boy in the picture was the same boy that they had just seen sitting in the car which was now empty of its passenger and motionless in the building which was deserted apart from the two men and the dog.

Max put his hand on Charlie's shoulder. "We won't be opening today, mate. Let's get out of here."

Charlie agreed and, as they exited the building, his phone sounded. He took it out of his pocket and read the text. It was from a number that he didn't recognise but it looked very official. It was from a law company called 'White, Grey, Black & Co. Solicitors' and it read like this:

Dear Mr Clementine,

You are cordially invited to attend the reading of the last will and testament of the late Ms Josie White at our office in Lydd, Kent. We feel that this would be in your best interests and on your acceptance, we will forward the appropriate details of time and location onto you.

Yours faithfully

White, Grey, Black & Co. Solicitors

His first thought was that it was a scam but then again, after what he had just witnessed in the ghost train, he was ready to believe that anything could be true. He put the phone back in his pocket and turned to Max who was locking the door of the building.

"I think we deserve a pint, mate," said Charlie.

Max agreed and they quickly headed off in the direction of the Golden Ball.

CHAPTER 3
YELLOW

York is a very interesting and atmospheric city at any time of the year. It is an ancient place which is steeped in a bloody history, and it is renowned for its many tales of ghostly sightings and supernatural phenomenon. Saffron Simpson was no stranger to York, having visited there many times over the years and on this occasion, she was there to compile a guidebook for the local tourist information centre who had invited her to write a short but comprehensive guide regarding the specific haunted buildings and ghosts in the area, of which there were many. She wasn't really doing it for the money, she just wanted people to take it away for free and enjoy the information, whether they believed it or not, a bit like a Gideon bible left in a hotel room. She had never seen a ghost herself but had always been interested in the subject, and her natural curiosity about all of the unexplained things that occur in the world had led her into her current job as a freelance journalist and part time author.

Saffron had spent most of the morning exploring Clifford's Tower, a castle that was sited at the top of a small hill and which, at this time of the year, was always overgrown with a multitude of beautiful daffodils.

e was a particular macabre story relating to the wer that dated back to 1190, when the 150-strong Jewish community of the city were trapped there by the local population because of the intense anti-Jewish feeling amongst the people at the time. Realising that there would be no escape or mercy from the angry mob outside, the Chief Rabbi had ordered that they all commit mass suicide, so the head of the households meticulously set about murdering the members of their own families. A handful of the community did manage to escape, only to be unfortunately set upon and brutally killed by the enraged mob outside. Saffron had grimaced at this image and thought of how appalling it must be to be murdered by a member of your own family and hoped that it was a fate that would never befall her.

She was now sitting having lunch inside a very old public house which was called Ye Olde Starre Inne. She was picking away at lemon sole with salad and chips, while she listened to the music that was being piped into the bar room. It was quite a dated playlist, which had so far included Yellow River by Christie and a song that Tony Orlando used to sing called Tie a Yellow Ribbon Round the Old Oak Tree, and she couldn't help but smile to herself when Donovan sang his opening line to Mellow Yellow when he mentioned his liking of Saffron. She finished off her meal and left the establishment and started walking up the narrow street, called Stonegate, in the direction of the majestic cathedral-like structure of York Minster, which she intended to visit next.

She stopped at the bay window of a tiny shop, which was simply called The Antique Shop. She hadn't noticed it ever before and was curious as to why, so she decided to go inside for a browse around. As she stepped through the doorway, it was immediately obvious that the exterior of the shop was a total deception of what lay inside. The internal space was immense, just like the Tardis in Doctor Who and, as she was about to find out, as she travelled through her own personal journey of time and relative distance in space exploration inside the shop, the treasures that lay within were mind-boggling. The place was more like a museum than a mere shop. The door closed behind her to the ring of a brass doorbell, and she immediately noticed that there didn't appear to be any people in the place apart from a young girl shop assistant. She stood behind a counter in the middle of the shop, busily working on paperwork of some description but when the bell rang, she looked up and smiled at Saffron.

The shop itself was greater in length than it was in width, but it was jam-packed with glass display cabinets, which in turn were chock a block with all kinds of antique and vintage items. There was everything from jewellery, watches, roman relics, fossils, pottery of all descriptions, coins, stamps and all types of old toys and general bric-a-brac. The floor space was festooned with statues, furniture, garden ornaments and all sorts of paraphernalia. On the walls hung paintings, drawings, photographs, tapestries, old maps, and framed embroidery. Saffron slowly started to make her way forward, trying to take it all in, which proved to be an impossible task as there was just too much to look at and contemplate. As she neared the shop assistant, she said, "You've got so much stuff in here… it's quite amazing."

"I know," said the young woman, who looked like she was in her twenties. "But it doesn't all belong to us, we're like the middleman who sells the stuff on behalf of other dealers."

"Oh, I see," said Saffron. "It's such a big place as well, really deceiving from the outside."

"Yeah, and there's also a basement level and a first floor which has a café."

"Oh my God!" exclaimed Saffron. "I better crack on exploring then."

The young woman smiled at her. "Take your time. There's no rush," she added.

Saffron carried on with her perusal of the stock and left the girl behind as she proceeded through the labyrinth of the shop. There had been many things that had caught her eye, but one thing in particular had been an amber brooch in the shape of a canary which had two real yellow feathers attached to it and it was only twelve pounds. She had made a mental note of its position and decided if she didn't see anything else to tempt her, she would buy it. She reached the top of a staircase and descended into the basement section. These rooms were full of old military gear, from uniforms and helmets to swords and muskets and everything in between. There was also a section of retro clothes of all descriptions from all eras, and Saffron was surprised to stumble upon the young woman who was now arranging a fur coat on one of the mannequins. She had obviously come down here from another entrance because she had definitely not passed Saffron on the way.

"Hello again," Saffron offered.

"Hi, have you seen anything you like yet?"

"Well, there is a lovely amber brooch upstairs that I have my eye on, but I'll wait until I've seen everything. Or almost everything." She laughed and went back up the stairs and it wasn't long before she was ascending another staircase to the first floor. Here she found the café, which was called Molly's Tea Rooms and, once again to her surprise, here was the young woman, this time behind the food counter and wearing a white apron.

"Gosh, you get around, don't you?"

"I know my way about and knew that you would head up here," said the young woman, smiling.

"Is there nobody else working here today?" asked Saffron.

"No, just me at the moment. You see, it doesn't usually get busy until later on in the day," she explained. "Would you like anything to eat or drink? We've got toasted teacakes, scones with jam and cream. I could even make you the omelette of the day if you would like."

"That's very kind of you," said Saffron. "I've actually just eaten but thanks for offering. However, I think that I've made my mind up about the brooch. I'll have another quick look around and I'll let you know."

"That's fine, be my guest." And with that, she carried on with cleaning the food counter and organising the coffee cups.

Saffron didn't waste much time and after a brief look at the first-floor offerings, she made her way downstairs to the cabinet with the brooch. To her dismay and utter bemusement, when she looked inside the cabinet, she realised that the brooch was no longer there.

"That can't be," she said to herself. "I'm the only customer here."

"Don't worry, I've already taken it out for you," shouted the now familiar voice of the young woman from her original position behind the cash register. Saffron spun around to see her holding up the brooch in her hand and smiling her seemingly permanent smile.

"You had me worried there for a minute. I thought someone had beaten me to it," said Saffron, and they both laughed.

"It's a unique piece. You can tell by the individual hallmark on the back, see." The woman turned the brooch over in her hand and showed Saffron the mark, which also had the initials JW clearly engraved upon it.

"Oh, yes!" exclaimed Saffron who then paid the twelve pounds and decided to wear it immediately on the lapel of her jacket.

The young woman pinned it on for her and Saffron admired herself in the reflection of one of the glass cabinets.

"Well, thank you very much, it's been an absolute pleasure visiting your shop."

"You're more than welcome and don't forget to tell all your friends."

"No chance," laughed Saffron. "They might come and buy all the good stuff before me and that will never do."

And so, to the sounds of each other's laughter, Saffron bade her farewell and left the shop. She had only walked a dozen paces up the street when she stopped in the realisation that she had meant to ask the woman for a business card for future reference. Saffron doubled back, but when she reached the shop, she was met with the most confusing and disturbing sight. The small bay window, which had been adorned and dressed with shiny ornaments and jewellery, was now empty of anything apart from spider webs and dead wasps and flies. She peered through the window into the darkness of a building that was now empty of any display cabinets or anything at all. Desperately she rattled the door handle, but it was locked shut.

It was then that an elderly gentleman who was passing by noticed what she was trying to do. He stopped and said to her, "You won't be able to get in there, luv, it's been shut for donkey's years. You'll be better off trying somewhere else. There's lots of antique shops in York."

"But…" Saffron began and then pulled herself up short, deciding not to tell the man what she had been doing for the best part of the last hour as she would sound quite insane.

She glanced down at her jacket lapel. Amazingly, the brooch was still there, but now the metal clasp was tarnished, the feathers tattered and faded, then as she peered into the void of the empty shop window, her phone pinged. Still dazed by the inexplicable experience that she had just had, she took the phone out of her pocket and read the text. It was from a company called White, Grey,

Black & Co. Solicitors, and although she didn't know it, it was just like the text that Richard Redman and Charlie Clementine had received and it said:

Dear Miss Simpson,

You are cordially invited to attend the reading of the last will and testament of the late Ms Josie White at our office in Lydd, Kent. We feel that this would be in your best interests and on your acceptance, we will forward the appropriate details of time and location onto you.

Yours faithfully

White, Grey, Black & Co. Solicitors

She put the phone back into her pocket and glanced at the shop for one last time and then walked away. As she did so, the ghostly face of a young smiling woman appeared in the first floor window, watching as Saffron headed off in the direction of York Minster.

CHAPTER 4
GREEN

"Gave a load of veg to the food bank the other day," said Emma Reldin as she teased a weed from one of the many flower beds.

"Who did?" enquired Jade, her friend, who was on the other end of the phone.

"I did. I thought that it would be a nice gesture. I mean, we've got enough here to feed the five thousand."

"Well, that's true and very kind of you as well. Look, I'm coming up the drive now, so I'll see you in two ticks, alright."

"No probs, you know where I am." Emma placed the phone in the front pocket of her denim dungarees as Jade parked her car on the other side of the expansive walled garden.

Emma had been working at Mulgrave Castle near Lythe, which is just above Sandsend near Whitby, for many years and was now employed as the head gardener. The whole estate was a staggering 16,000 acres and extremely popular with the rich and famous during the four-month game bird shooting season. Most of the area was managed by the gamekeepers and groundsmen and it was Emma's job to maintain and cultivate everything inside the walled garden, as well as the impressive fruit orchard next door.

It was the Friday before the May Day Bank Holiday weekend, which would see the Castle gardens, orchard and grounds opened up to the public and, as always, Emma's friend Jade was coming along to help her with the final preparations. Emma looked up as the metal latch on the old wooden door snicked open and in walked Jade, who was dressed appropriately in working clothes and boots with her sleeves already rolled up, her hair tied back with a headscarf.

"Right, where would you like me to start?" Jade asked as she purposefully walked towards Emma.

"Well, you can start by helping me to finish this bit of weeding off and then there's loads to do after that." Jade knelt down next to Emma and got stuck into the task.

"Thanks for coming by the way. I really appreciate it, you know," said Emma

"Not a problem," responded Jade. "You know I love coming here, especially at this time of the year when everything's in bloom. It's beautiful."

"It sure is," agreed Emma. "It's also bloody hard work to keep it like that as you know. Blood, sweat and tears."

"You know the score, sister… no pain, no gain."

"Don't I know it." They both laughed as they continued with the weeding. "A lot of people will be looking forward to seeing their relatives at this time but I'm looking forward to seeing that hoverfly that comes in the garden every year, who I've named Hector by the way, and that little blue butterfly who always turns up."

"Can't be the same ones every year surely?" Jade asked doubtfully.

"Well, you come back every year and you're the same one," replied Emma, who was laughing her head off.

"I don't know, you are strange sometimes, Miss Reldin, you really are."

"Well, who wants to be normal anyway?" asked Emma.

"Normal people, I suppose," offered Jade.

"Well, good luck to them. Live and let live, that's what I say and never the twain shall meet. I'm quite happy living my slightly eccentric lifestyle and I ain't changing for nobody. They can do their thing and I'll do mine and if people don't like it, then tough."

Jade just smiled at her friend and carried on with the work in hand. Despite the huge amount of time, dedication and attention to detail that she gave to her job, Emma also managed to find time to perform with the local amateur dramatic society who were known as the Stiddy Players. She was often cast in the role of an oddball character and always played the part to the best of her ability, which was actually very good. The company had taken their name from a local tradition, whereby the top of a blacksmith's anvil would be loaded with gunpowder and then set alight with a taper that resulted in an obviously impressive explosion just like the firing of a cannon. The anvil was located at the forge just outside of the Castle's entrance from the village, which Jade had just driven through, and the ceremony had been performed often over many decades.

Emma was pleased that her friend was here, not just to

help her out but to also keep her company, because over the last couple of days when she had been working alone, she had the uneasy feeling that she was being watched by some unseen presence. The current building, Mulgrave Castle, was actually the third castle that had been built on the estate and was actually a castellated mansion house built to replace the previous Norman castle that was built in 1120 and garrisoned by Royalists during the English civil war before being dismantled by Parliamentary order in 1647. Going further back in time, the ruins of the original castle, which was allegedly built by Wada, the ruler of Haslingland, who was supposedly a 'giant', could be clearly seen below, from the orchard, on the other side of the valley. The place was steeped in history and the house had even been used as a convalescent home for recovering veterans both during and after the First World War.

"Okay, we're finished here now so I'm going over there to sort the veggies out if you want to go and see if any of the roses need attention," Emma said.

"Yeah, no worries," replied Jade, and she took a pair of secateurs out of Emma's basket to carry along with her trowel and fork, and she wandered over to the section of the garden which housed the many rose bushes.

While she was on her own, Emma's thoughts began to wonder about the power of the force of nature and the fact that nature abhors a vacuum. Over time, nature eventually reclaims all things that are man-made, just like it does with our own mortal bodies. There are countless examples all over the world, like ancient temples in the jungles of South America, which have been totally incorporated into the structure of the surrounding vegetation, disused and abandoned chemical plants which now have trees and bushes actually growing out of the lagged cladding of vessels and pipework, the tarmacked roads having been split open by trees growing through the cracks of the surface and now suitably occupied by all kinds of wildlife like deer, rabbits and foxes. There are redundant fuel storage sites, which have huge petrol and diesel tanks with floating roofs, the roofs being lowered right down to the bottom of the inside of the vessels, which now contain their own ecosystems. You can climb up the spiral staircase that hugs the outside of the structure, then look down onto a scene of surreal woodland beauty, the whole space having been invaded by the biodiversity of the outside world. There are even ponds that have formed in the indentations on the roof's steel fabrication that are surrounded by bulrushes and home to various species of birds like waders, dippers, grey wagtails, and the occasional visiting heron, all of them secure in the knowledge that they are free from any mammalian predators. Emma recalled that once, on a visit to Saltburn, when she was walking down the road towards the cenotaph, she had come across a tree whose trunk had actually grown around the horizontal scaffold-like bar of the fence on the side of the pavement. Over a long period of time, the tree had absorbed the manmade object into itself. Eventually everything comes to pass, Emma thought. Everything has a beginning and an end. Even the entire human race will one day become extinct by some means or another, just like the dinosaurs. At the end of the day, we are all just brief visitors to this beautiful planet and that's the law of the jungle. She was snapped out of her thinking by Jade who had approached her with something in her hand.

"Look what I've found," she said.

"What is it?" asked Emma.

"Some kind of button, but it looks quite special. What do you think?" She held it out to Emma for inspection. It looked very old and was probably made of brass. The tarnish and the muck that was clinging to it made it difficult to clearly see the design, however she could make out a crown at the top with a cross underneath it and then the letters XIX, but beyond that everything else was unreadable. "Here, you take it." Jade passed the button to Emma who took it from her.

"Thanks," she said, "I'll clean it up later and get a better look at it." She put it in her front pocket and with that, they both carried on with the day's labours until Emma decided that enough was enough. She thanked Jade for her help as her friend climbed back into her car and watched her turn and head back up the driveway, the car's tyres crunching on the gravel surface. Emma's accommodation was not far away. She walked up the driveway, following Jade's vehicle, and quickly found herself walking besides a woodland area on her left. Soon she came to a gate in the fence and walked through it onto the path that led to the gardener's cottage, which was where she lived, and which was provided as part of the job. She entered the front door, locked it behind her then took a shower and put on her civvy clothes. In the kitchen, she peeled a selection of vegetables, put them in a pan and poured in a pint of stock and herbs. She lit the gas ring and placed the lid half-cocked on top of the pan. Emma was just about to make a cup of tea when someone knocked on the front door. She thought that it was probably one of the groundsmen come to ask her for some kind of favour, so she was very surprised when she opened the door to a young man who was probably in his twenties and who was dressed in khaki military clothing. He wore a full-length trench coat and a cap with an insignia on the front that Emma found vaguely familiar.

"I'm sorry to trouble you, ma'am, but my name's Howard Green and I was wondering if you have found the button off my coat. I think I lost it yesterday when I was walking through the garden." He pointed to his coat and gestured towards the walled garden with a quick turn and nod of his head. "I've seen you working in there the last few days and watched that young lady give you something earlier on and I was just wondering, on the off chance, whether or not it was my button."

Emma didn't know how to respond. Her brain couldn't compute what was being asked and she couldn't work out why this man, who she didn't recognise, would be here dressed like that. Then she suddenly remembered the button that Jade had given to her that morning.

In her confusion and without questioning, Emma said, "Wait here." She closed the door and retrieved the still dirty button from her dungarees and returned to open the door. "Is this the one you mean? I'm sorry I haven't

123

had time to clean it up yet." She gave the button, which looked very similar to the other shiny ones on his coat, to the soldier who placed it in the missing space on his coat in order to show her that it was indeed the one.

"Yes, that's it. Thank you, I won't get into bother now." And before she had the chance to respond he turned and walked up the path, with a pronounced limp, to the gate, where he stopped and said, "Are you coming to watch them fire the Stiddy?"

"When?" she asked.

"Very shortly. They're getting it ready now."

"Why are they firing it today?" she enquired.

"For King George's birthday, of course," the soldier replied through his broad smile.

"King George?" Emma was very confused now and then the soldier burst out laughing.

"George the Fifth, of course, ma'am. Who else would it be?" He turned, exited through the gate and continued to walk up the driveway in the direction of the blacksmiths.

Emma shut the door and went to turn off the pan which was simmering away on the stove. The only logical explanation that she could think of was that they must be doing some kind of historical recreation, and as for the button, she was sure that Jade had stitched her up with one of her practical jokes. Having only seen the 'Firing of the Stiddy' on two occasions, she was keen to get in on the action, so she locked the front door behind herself and headed for the drive entranceway.

When she reached the forge, the place was deserted. It had all been locked up for the day and there was nobody around. The anvil was not outside and there was no sign of the young soldier. She felt a shiver of anxiety run down her spine as she looked around for an explanation as to what might be going on, but there were no clues forthcoming. She actually felt quite embarrassed, and so it was with a troubled mind that she quickly made her way back to the cottage.

Before she had the chance to turn the stove back on, the text alert on her phone sounded. It was from a group of solicitors down in Kent who were inviting her to the reading of the will of somebody called Josie White. Emma had never heard of Josie White before and so treated the message with scant regard. She put the phone down and relit the gas ring. As she stood staring at the mixture of vegetables in the soup, Emma perused the possibilities of an explanation for her visitation by the unknown warrior. The soup began to boil, and she could only come to one conclusion… which was that she had seen a ghost.

CHAPTER 5
BLUE

"Battle of Bosworth Field was fought on the 22nd of August 1485," explained Stanley Blumenthal to his dog Henry, who was a Staffordshire Blue. They were both walking down a path through the woods towards Saltburn Viaduct, which spans the valley, allowing the passage of railway freight from one side to the other and which is predominantly used nowadays for the transportation of potash from the mine at Boulby.

He often walked through the woods in order to get out of the house after the recent death of his beloved wife, the house being a quiet and lonely place now. Stanley was currently revising for a charity mastermind competition which was to be held at the Leven Street Mission Church where he was a regular attendee. His chosen specialised subject was going to be the War of the Roses, which had been fought between the Yorkists and the Lancastrians during the fifteenth century and, seeing as there was nobody else around, he had decided to speak the answers out loud, not just for Henry's education but to also add gravitas to the facts in his memory. As they descended the pathway, Stanley began to recall a memory from over fifty years ago when he had made this journey before as a young boy. He must have been about eleven or twelve years old, he reckoned at the time which was back in the early 1960s. He knew that at the end of this path, when it reached the bottom of the valley, there was a junction and a choice of whether to go right and walk under the monolithic red brick arch of the viaduct structure towards the waterfall or take a left on a less trodden route. When they reached the intersection, Stanley stopped and began to recall the details of the strange occurrence that had happened to him all of those years ago.

•

The young Stanley Blumenthal loved the outdoors and any chance that he got he would head through the woods into the valley towards Skelton Beck in order to fish for the wild brown trout that were indigenous to the stream. The wild brownies were distinguishable from the alien rainbow trout because of the pattern of red dots on their flanks, unlike the pinkish rainbow-like hue of the other species. Once in a blue moon, he would unfortunately catch a freshwater eel. These fish inhabited their lairs that were called haunts, which would be a tangle of submerged roots and branches from deadfall trees that had been washed downstream. The eel would fight with the strength of a demon, which always resulted in one of two outcomes, either the line would become totally snagged within the labyrinth of its haunt, or the fish would be landed. Either of these results always required the same conclusion, which was to cut the line because, even if the fish was landed, the eel inevitably would have swallowed the hook, making it impossible to be disgorged. Stanley had also often caught small flatfish in the beck, which always amazed him as he didn't associate the species with freshwater, and he was convinced that their place in nature was in the sea. His best catch however, had been a migratory sea trout which he had measured at twenty-one inches long and, because he was sympathetic to the fact that the creature was obviously on its return journey upstream to the spawning grounds where it had been hatched after maybe travelling thousands of miles through the oceans, he had released it back into the water alive and unharmed.

It was the month of May and the woodland had burst into bloom. Everything was growing and the birds were singing with the joy that springtime brings, a time of renewal and rebirth. He could hear a woodpecker drumming its beak into a tree trunk somewhere in the depths of the woods and he observed a nuthatch clinging to the side of a tree, pecking at the insects that were resident on the bark. A grey squirrel ran across the path in front of him and he remembered the other animals that he been lucky to see during his visits to the area. Very early one morning, he had turned the corner leading into the meadow just below the Italian Gardens and then stopped dead in his tracks as in front of him, only about thirty yards away was a stag, just standing there with its ears twitching. They maintained the 'Mexican Standoff' for what seemed like ages, until the deer finally realised that he was being watched by a human, whereby he quickly turned and leapt into the undergrowth, crashing through the ferns and flora eventually to disappear completely from view and earshot. Strangely, it was on the same morning, about an hour later at a spot in the beck which was aptly named The Beaver Dam, that an otter emerged from the stream in front of him and sat on a rock ledge for a few seconds, only a matter of feet away, before diving back into the water and swimming downstream and finally out of sight. Stanley had seen numerous water voles over the months who always announced their presence with an audible plop as they plunged into the stream and swam to the opposite bank, but seeing an otter was a first for him. Another first had been the time when he had witnessed a lightning flash of electric blue as the undeniable image of a kingfisher darted past him with its beautifully coloured plumage and long beak.

Today however, after just embarking on his descent down into the woods, he first needed to hunt for a different kind of creature. He had to dig for earthworms, which in his mind were a killer bait for the wild brownies. On both sides of the path, the woodland floor was carpeted with the white flowers of the wild garlic plants and the overwhelming pungent aroma of garlic filled the air. Stanley left the path and walked several feet into the wood and then he took a gardening fork out of his fishing bag, which incidentally had been his grandad's gas mask bag during the Second World War, and he started digging. Stanley mused that he could do with wearing a gas mask now actually as the smell of uprooted garlic bulbs and freshly dug earth were proving to be quite intoxicating.

After a short while, he was confident that he had enough juicy worms in his bait tin for today's fishing session and so he set off to a place called The Fairy Glen, where he was going to start his campaign, travelling downstream through the Italian gardens towards the boating lake, which was the small estuary of the burn where the freshwater eventually finished its journey by flowing across the sandy beach and into the salty North Sea.

On reaching his chosen fishing mark, he quickly assembled his gear, then stealthily, so as not to spook the fish, approached a part of the stream where a small run of rapids entered a deep meandering pool. He dangled the hook with the worm on it into the fast flow and started to let out line from his centre pin reel. The worm and attached waggler float, which was like a six-inch-long stick, were immediately taken downstream by the fast-flowing current and deposited into the pool where the flow of water was much slower. Stanley continued to let out line in order to allow the bait to travel in a natural way, and a few seconds later the float, which had been lying horizontal on the surface of the water, ceased its journey and stood upright. Then in a flash, it disappeared underneath the water.

He quickly struck the rod backwards and straight away felt the undeniable thumping of a fish on the other end of the line. He reeled in under control so he could play the fish towards him and away from the snags on the other side of the bank.

130

Soon there was a flash of silver in the stream, and he knew that he had a trout on the hook. Very carefully, he brought the fish in and gently hauled it onto the beach-like bank where he was standing. It was a wild brownie, exactly the species that he had been targeting and it was often the case that the first cast into a 'run' would be the most productive.

He unhooked the small fish, marvelling at the colours of its scales and, realising that it was undersized, he placed it back into the water and gently held it until it had regained its strength enough to swim away into the depths. Inspired by his early success, he continued downstream, stopping whenever he found a promising looking stretch of water into which he could trot the bait.

His next spot of luck came when he caught another brownie at a bend in the beck that was situated just before the location of the towering structure of the Ha'penny Bridge, which also spanned the valley just like the viaduct further upstream. This bridge however, had been made out of cast iron and wood and completed in 1867, unfortunately with the loss of three lives, to allow the passage of pedestrians and horses and carts rather than steam trains. Some years later in 1974, the bridge would be demolished due to its deterioration and lack of funding to maintain the structure. The story itself would even make the national news on television, which would feature footage of the exploding legs on the collapsing iconic landmark and it would prove very sad to watch.

Just before he reached the boating lake, he came to the decision, because it was still early in the morning, that he would try his luck at an area of the beck that he had never explored before. He started walking back upstream from where he had just travelled and ascended up through the Italian Gardens to the pathways in the woodland above. From here, he followed the track that eventually led him to the junction below the viaduct. He had fished in the waterfall beyond the viaduct twice but had never taken the left turn around the bend, so this morning he decided to venture into unknown territories.

He turned left and walked around the corner of the undergrowth. As he did so, he noticed that curiously there was a manmade stone channel of flowing water that was running in a ditch by his left-hand side. On completion of the turn, a marvellous view came into sight.

There were a number of buildings clustered together in an idyllic rural setting, most of them looked like farm buildings or workshops and three of them looked like silos or storehouses. These were cylindrical in construction, two of them having dome shaped roofs and the largest having a conical roof. But the most striking and unusual structure was a very large detached Victorian house to the right of the settlement. It looked totally out of place down here in the deep wooded valley, but its presence was an obvious indication that this must be a going concern of one form or another. The smoke that was coming from the chimney was an indication that someone was at home and, as he walked onwards, he first heard and then saw to the left-hand corner of the small holding, a large wooden waterwheel that was rotating at a good pace. It then became obvious that this was a working mill but why hadn't he been aware of its existence before now?

The scene before him was quite surreal and he soon realised that in order to access the stream beyond, he would have to walk through the yard of the property, which was fenced off and obviously private. He stopped at the latched gate and listened to the grinding of the millstones as he pondered what to do next. It was then that a young girl appeared, walking from behind of one of the silos. She immediately saw him, and she began to approach. She was wearing a navy blue dress and Stanley guessed that she was maybe a couple of years older than him. She stopped at the other side of the gate, her long blonde ringlets of curly hair framing her attractive facial features, and when she smiled, her whole face lit up and her bright blue eyes twinkled.

"Hello," she said. "I've never seen you down here before."

"I didn't even know that this place existed," admitted Stanley.

"Oh yes, we've been down here a long time."

"Do you live here?" he enquired.

"Yes, with my family. We run the mill." She glanced down at the fishing rod in his hand. "Are you going fishing?"

"Yes, I was hoping to be able to get down there." He pointed to the area beyond the compound. "But it would mean having to cross your yard."

"That's alright, you can come in." She unlatched the gate and swung it open.

"Thanks," said Stanley as he entered the property.

"My name's Veronica, by the way," the girl informed him.

"Nice to meet you. I'm Stanley."

"Follow me, Stanley. I'll show you the way," said Veronica as she closed the gate behind them.

There was something about the way that she looked at him as she walked past that actually caused his heart to miss a beat and a warm flush of intense emotion to fill his entire body. He had felt this way a couple of times before with a few of the girls at school, but it had never been this overwhelming. He followed her past the silos, where the chickens, geese and ducks were pecking at the ground. As they passed the magnificent house, he could smell the aroma of baking coming from an open window, which must have been the kitchen.

Presently they stopped at the far end of the yard, and Stanley could now hear the flow of the stream beyond the edge of the wood in front of them.

"It's just down there," said Veronica, pointing to a narrow path that disappeared into the dense undergrowth. "Here, take these for good luck." She handed him the posy of fresh bluebells that she had been carrying. "I just picked them before you arrived."

"Thank you." He took the flowers from her and as he did, their hands briefly brushed together, at which point he thought he was going to faint.

"You're welcome to come through here anytime, Stanley. And I'd really like to see you again."

"Thank you. I will come back soon." And, as he placed

the flowers into the top of his fishing bag, he looked at her and added, "I promise."

At that, she grinned from ear to ear and once again Stanley was almost moved to tears at her attractiveness. He turned and walked towards the path.

"Goodbye," said Veronica.

"Bye for now," replied Stanley and, as he glanced back over his shoulder, Veronica was waving to him, and he nearly tripped head over heels when she blew him a kiss and then giggled like a mischievous imp. Soon though she was gone from sight and Stanley found himself standing at the water's edge thinking to himself, 'I think I'm in love.'

The most striking feature of this part of the watercourse was the set of stepping-stones that straddled the width of the beck, allowing him to easily cross to the other side. Once across, he immediately began to fish, having already got a worm on the hook from before which was still full of life. He fished the deep gulley, which looked very promising, with unfortunately no bites. It was from here that his plan was to follow the beck downstream all the way to where he had started that morning at the Fairy Glen. This part of the valley resembled a canyon, with steep cliffs of sedimentary stone flanking either side of the stream. Stanley observed that at this point, for the journey to continue, he would have to get up onto higher ground for a while before coming back down to the water. He scoured the unfamiliar area for a route of escape and soon found a small trackway that led up the side of the bank. Stanley ascended the trail and then found himself in an open ancient woodland where the floor was carpeted wall to wall with a beautiful covering of bluebells.

'This is where Veronica must have picked the flowers earlier on,' Stanley thought to himself.

It really was a peaceful and tranquil area with the busy sound of the beck below having been replaced with the earnest songs of the many resident birds. The sun was streaming in shafts of light through the dense foliage of the trees, which illuminated patches of bluebells just like spotlights. As he progressed through the woodland, Stanley realised that he was getting higher, and this particular route was taking him further away from where he wanted to be. It soon became apparent that he was going to really struggle to find a safe way back down to the beck, so after a few minutes he reluctantly decided to retrace his steps all the way back to the mill and from there he would either try and find another access route on the opposite side of the stream or just call it a day.

He crossed the stepping-stones and ascended up the narrow pathway that would lead him into the yard of the mill but when he emerged from the woods, he stopped dead in his tracks and his blood ran icy cold.

All the buildings had vanished.

Everything had gone, apart from a couple of short, ruined stone walls which were overgrown with ivy to his right, and to his left just a small mound of rubble where the house had been standing just half an hour ago. The waterwheel no longer existed, and the entire area was just grass, nettles, and bramble bushes.

A cold breeze then rose out of nowhere, which

practically took his breath away and engulfed him in sadness. Confused and dazed, Stanley was rooted to the spot in disbelief, but the most disturbing element of it all was the dawning realisation that he would never see Veronica again. That revelation quickly took over his thought process as the tears slowly began to flow down his face. Then a glimmer of hope as he remembered the posy of bluebells in his bag that she had given him. Surely if they were real then she must be real too. He quickly pulled back the flap of the bag and then his world fell apart as he pulled out the wilted brown remains of the not-so-long-ago fresh flowers and their pathetic remains crumbled to dust in his hand. This, in turn, was carried away and scattered by the wind. It was then that he panicked, and he sprinted out of the clearing onto the woodland path. Running as fast as he could up the steep incline, with the muscles in his legs burning and suffering the agony of stitches in his sides, he wondered what kind of cruel joke had occurred or what kind of evil influence had been at work down below in the isolated solitude of the woods and so he made a mental note never to return there.

•

The much older Stanley Blumenthal and his dog Henry stood paused at the junction of the pathways and he thought about his wife's last words a month ago as she lay on her deathbed, holding his hand. She had battled hard against the cancer that had ravaged her body, but she knew now that it was time for her to depart and she had whispered the strangest thing to him.

"Please don't leave any promises unfulfilled, Stan. I love you." And with that, she left him.

And that was the reason for him standing here now. He had never visited this place again after the strange events of years ago but with his wife's last request fresh in his thoughts, and being mindful of the fact that there were more mysteries between the wild blue yonder and the deep blue sea than any human brain could understand or begin to comprehend, he put one foot forward and began the walk around the corner to the left.

He noticed that there was no water flowing in the stone trough of the millrace like there had been before and that it was full of plants and broken in many places. He wasn't quite sure what he would find, but his heart sank when he turned the corner and saw the wasteland before him. It was even more overgrown than before, with the pile of rubble from the house having been completely covered with nettles and thick bramble bushes. There were even about a dozen sapling trees that had taken root and grown quite tall. The whole area was covered in grasses, wildflowers, and weeds but he still walked forward and, as Henry followed obediently behind him, Stanley made his way to the path that would lead him down to the stream.

The narrow track was still there, and he stood before it, wondering if the stepping-stones were still in place. He walked forward but had only taken a few paces into the dense undergrowth when Henry starting barking very enthusiastically somewhere behind him. Thinking that he must have seen a squirrel or a rabbit, Stanley turned back to check on the dog and he re-emerged from the trail. The image before him was amazing, he even stopped breathing for a while as he took in the scene.

The smallholding was back exactly as it had been the first time that he had come here. The three silos stood tall, with the geese, chickens and ducks foraging around in the dirt of the yard floor for whatever scraps of seeds and food that they could find. The outbuildings were all there again, as was the mill itself with the waterwheel rotating strongly in an anti-clockwise direction. The sounds of the water falling, and the grinding of the millstones, filled the air. To his left, the detached house stood proud with smoke emitting from its chimney and then the front door opened. It was Veronica and she was calling back to somebody who was inside the house.

"I won't be long. I just need to talk to him. I haven't seen him for ages." She left the front doorstep and ran down the path and through the open gate towards Stanley and when she reached him, she stopped and gazed upwards into his eyes. She hadn't changed a bit, unlike Stanley, and her blue eyes still blazed with the radiance of her youth. She had a huge grin on her face and then she spoke. "You actually came back to visit me."

Stanley was now totally mystified as to what was happening but was more than happy to play along with it as he was now feeling those warm waves of emotion that he had felt when he had stood here before as a young boy. He cleared his throat and began to speak.

"Veronica, I am so happy to see you again but are you really real or am I dreaming you?"

She smiled again and then, standing on her tiptoes, she placed a hand on his shoulder and craned her neck up to him, whereby she kissed him tenderly on the cheek. He could feel the warmth of her lips and the soft breath on his face.

"Did that feel real?" she asked him and then giggled.

He had to agree that it had felt very real indeed.

"I am sorry about your wife, Stanley. I know that you loved each other very much but she is in a safe and happy place now and she sends her love to you."

Stanley wondered how she knew these things, but he let her continue.

"Look, I've brought you a present to cheer you up." And from behind her back, she produced a bunch of forget-me-not flowers.

He took the posy from her, and they brushed hands as they had before. Stanley thanked her and then a woman's voice called out from the house.

"Veronica, your dinner's ready. Don't let it go cold."

"I have to go now. That's my mam shouting me. Thanks for coming to see me again."

"It was really great to see you and thanks again for the flowers."

"Don't ever forget me, will you?" Veronica pleaded as she turned on her heels and ran to the garden gate of the house where she stopped, turned, and blew him another kiss. She ran to the front door, giggling all the way, and when she finally closed it behind her, everything instantly vanished. The overgrown wasteland returned, and that icy wind reappeared which chilled him to the bone.

He looked down at the flowers he was holding, and he wasn't surprised to see that once again they had wilted like before; they turned to dust and dispersed on the breeze.

Henry emerged from underneath a bush and came running up to him.

"Come on, pal, it's time to go home." Unlike the first time, Stanley did not panic, he just casually strolled out of the clearing with Henry and they made their way back to their home in Montrose Street.

He opened the front door and picked up a letter from the doormat. It looked official as it had a stamp of a solicitors on it, which read White, Grey, Black & Co. He entered the house, sat down, opened the envelope and read the contents. He had never heard of Josie White which made him curious but for now he put the letter to one side and picked up a framed photograph of his wife instead. He stared into her eyes and as he did so, a single teardrop dripped from his cheek and splashed onto the glass of the photo frame.

CHAPTER 6
INDIGO

"In the beginning God created the heaven and the earth. And the earth was without form, and void; and darkness was on the face of the deep. And the spirit of God moved upon the face of the waters. And God said, let there be light." Ian Drago spoke the words as he finished replacing the lightbulb that had blown.

He then turned and flicked the light switch on the wall and when the bulb instantly came to life, he declared, "And there was light." He laughed a self-satisfied laugh and then carried on restocking the bottles behind the bar. Ian was the owner and landlord of a pub called Indigo Alley, located on the North Marine Road in Scarborough.

"Do you believe in ghosts?" asked Sandra the cleaner as she continued to polish the surface of one of the many tables.

"No, I'm a bit of a sceptic when it comes to that kind of thing," he admitted. "Although there is a law in physics, which says that matter can neither be created nor destroyed. Which I suppose means that everything and

142

everyone has to come back eventually as something else, somewhere else. Why do you ask?"

"It's just that strange things keep happening in here when I'm cleaning."

"What kind of things?" Ian was curious to know.

"Well, the other day when you hadn't come downstairs yet, I'd finished in the bar, so I went to start on the loos. When I got there, I realised that I'd left my cleaning stuff behind in the bar, so I came back in and six of the tables had a single chair on the top. I'd only been gone a few seconds and I know that I had put them all on the floor after I'd finished hoovering like I always do, and the chairs weren't turned upside down, they were all the right way round. It was really spooky."

"That's really weird. Are you sure there was nobody else in here? Maybe playing a practical joke," he enquired.

"I'm positive, and anyway, they wouldn't have had time, it would be impossible. You do believe me, don't you?"

"I believe you, Sandra, but I just can't offer an explanation for it," he told her.

"And there's been other things as well. Sometimes doors open and close on their own, and I've seen shadows moving and heard footsteps and people talking and whispering when the pub's been empty."

Ian cleared his throat and then spoke. "Well, look, I've lived and worked here for quite a few years now and I've never seen or heard anything."

"Hmm, well, I'm not convinced. I think something's going on. Something *paranormal*."

And with that, they both went back to their tasks. Ian concluded that Sandra had an overactive imagination. She did like watching her horror films late at night as well as all that other supernatural rubbish that they put on the telly nowadays.

"Right," said Ian, "I'm done for now in here so I'm going out the back into the office to finish off tonight's quiz."

"Okay, but don't make the questions too hard like you did last week. I mean, give us a chance."

Ian laughed and, as he disappeared into the office, he shouted back to her, "Sandra, you even get the easy ones wrong."

"Cheeky sod," she shouted back.

Ian sat down at the computer and signed in. He glanced at the notepad that he had been scribbling on and then he began typing.

Q6: There used to be an exhibit in the Boston Zoo in America that had the title of 'The Most Dangerous Animal in the World'. What was the exhibit and what was the animal? And you get a point for each answer.
A: The exhibit was a mirror and so the animal of course was a human being, or yourself.

Ian laughed and moved onto the next question.

Half an hour later, Sandra peered around the doorway to the office. "I'm done for the day," she said, "so, if there's nothing else, I'll see you tonight."

"Yeah, that's fine," replied Ian, and then smiled as he

added, "Thanks, Sandra, and good luck for tonight, I think you might need it."

"I'll show you one of these days, you just watch. I've got a funny feeling that I'm going to win tonight and that'll wipe the smile off your face."

"I'll believe it when I see it," he said, shaking his head. "See you later."

"You sure will." She disappeared from the doorway and a few seconds later he heard the front door close.

After another hour of question compiling, he heard someone tapping on the bar trying to get some attention.

"Bloody hell," he cursed as he rose from behind the desk. "She's forgot to lock the door again." It was another twenty minutes until opening time, so he quickly left the office and went to the bar. On the other side, stood a young woman who was holding a clutch bag in front of her.

"Hello," he said. "Have you come about the barmaid's job?"

"No." She spoke with a quiet, nervous voice.

"Oh, well how can I help you? I mean, we don't open for another twenty minutes. The cleaner must have left the door unlocked again." He smiled.

"The door is locked," the woman stated.

"Then how did you get in?" Ian asked, quite alarmed.

She chose to ignore the question and then said, "I have come to warn you that you are in great danger and so is your brother."

"But I haven't got a brother!" he exclaimed.

"Yes, you have. He's your twin," she informed him.

"You've only met him once and that was on the day you were born."

"Look, I don't know if this is some kind of sick joke, pet, but I am very busy and we're not even open yet. So, come on, why are you saying all of this?"

"Because I am your mother," she calmly stated.

"Oh, come on, luv…" Ian was smiling now. "I must be three times older than you. So, what do you really want?"

"I died giving birth to the both of you, but I've been watching you for all of your life and I just had to come and tell you that soon you will be in great danger," she insisted.

"Right, enough is enough, you have to leave now." Ian fumbled for the keys in his pocket so that he could unlock the front door but only managed to drop them on the carpet. He bent down, retrieved them, and when he straightened up to his amazement the young woman had vanished.

"Hello?" he shouted out. "Hello?"

He walked quickly from behind the bar and scoured the room, even bending down to look beneath the tables. He checked the front door which was indeed locked, and he kept on calling hello as he rounded the corner into the other part of the bar room where the pool table was, but she wasn't there, so he headed for the toilets. He checked out both the gents and the ladies, making sure to open the cubicle doors in order to do a thorough search, but she was nowhere to be seen. And then he had a thought that maybe she had somehow distracted him so she could enter the office and steal the petty cash money that he kept in a drawer in his desk.

With a great sense of urgency, he re-entered the bar room and as he turned the corner, he came to a grinding halt. There in front of him on the top of the bar counter were six upturned pint glasses that had been stacked up in the shape of a triangle and underneath the lower middle glass he could clearly see a dog-eared photograph that had also been placed upside down. He tentatively approached the counter and disassembled the glass construction. He carefully picked up the photograph, which had a date written on it, which strangely enough was his birth date, and turned it over. It was a creased black and white photo which was obviously very old, but the most startling thing was the image that he was looking at. It was the young woman who he had just been talking to and she was laid on a hospital bed with her eyes closed and looking as white as a sheet. In each arm had been placed a small bundle of swaddling blankets which were obviously tiny babies, probably even new-borns.

It was then that a shocking thought struck him, which made him feel quite nauseous, and that was that the young woman in the photograph was actually dead.

He walked clumsily behind the bar and entered the office, where he sat down behind the desk, staring at the haunting image and thought about what the woman had told him. It certainly hadn't been a run of the mill conversation and he knew that he had been adopted shortly after he was born. His mam and dad had told him that just before his sixteenth birthday, but they had never mentioned anything about a twin brother. However, he did recall several curious events that had occurred over the years involving him strangely seeing himself in public places, like walking on the other side of the road or standing in a queue or just being part of the crowd down on the seafront. And oddly enough, he had been mistaken for someone else more than once, having been addressed as Charlie.

Did he have a doppelganger or a real-life twin?

He looked back at the photo and nearly fell off his chair when the woman opened her eyes and sat up in the hospital bed.

"You have a twin brother and shortly you will meet again but you are both in great danger, my son."

He threw the picture into the air and ran into the bar room. He hastily unlocked the front door and dashed outside. There was no way that he was going back in there alone and he decided to wait for Masie the barmaid to turn up to begin her shift.

As he was trying to calm down, something caught his eye. Unbelievably, in the road in front of him, a white van was slowly driving past, and you could have knocked him down with a feather when he observed the driver and realised that once again, he was looking at the spitting image of himself. He was too shocked to react as the van drove away so he just stood there in disbelief.

When Masie arrived, they both entered the pub and Ian returned to his office. The photograph was lying face down on the floor, so he picked it up without turning it over and quickly hid it underneath a stack of paperwork on his desk. He sat down, took a deep breath and, trying to push the thoughts of what had recently happened out of his mind, he endeavoured to finish off tonight's quiz.

He logged back in and immediately saw a notification for a newly received email. He clicked on it and read the contents. It was from a group of solicitors called White, Grey, Black & Co and they were inviting him to the reading of the last will and testament of Ms Josie White, who he had never heard of, down in Kent. He was about to press the delete button when suddenly he changed his mind. Maybe it wasn't a scam because it had appeared in his inbox and not the junk mail, so he decided to leave it where it was and gather his thoughts before he did anything else.

CHAPTER 7
VIOLET

"Vain you are, bloody vain." Iris Fishburn was talking to her partner who was sitting next to her in the passenger seat as they drove along in their battered old Transit van.

Violet Mainprize was looking in the mirror of the sun visor as she applied even more makeup to her already well decorated face.

"It's all about the image, baby," she explained to Iris.

"It's only a bloody practice, for Christ's sake," replied Iris.

"Yes, I know, but I've got to get into the zone. You know what I mean? So that I can find my mojo and do it with feeling."

Iris rolled her eyes and carried on driving them to the venue where they were going to have a 'loud' practice before their first proper gig on Friday night. They were the only two members in their band, The Sea Creatures, and their chosen style of music was mainly rock. Iris played the drums and Violet sang and played the electric violin, using a microphone headset instead of a microphone stand, as well as arranging all of the songs, and the result was quite impressive. They made a striking looking pair with Violet's theatrical stage makeup and long black hair along with Iris's shocking pink mohican. They both usually dressed in classic goth and steampunk styles and many of their friends had decided that they must be having a mid-life crisis. Today though was definitely a shorts and t-shirt day because of the intense heat. They had met at the Whitby Goth Weekend the previous October and had hit it off like a house on fire. Violet loved anything to do with the paranormal and totally connected with the weirdness of all the scary costumes. However, Iris was a total sceptic about supernatural things but was still drawn to the atmosphere of the occasion. They had soon formed a close relationship with each other and shortly afterwards they had moved into a rented cottage together in nearby Egton, close to the Witching Post Inn. Violet was a classically trained violinist and Iris was a very talented percussionist, so with their joint love of music, it had made perfect sense to form a band and have some serious fun with it. They had been working together on their repertoire for a couple of months now and had been satisfied enough with their progress to confidently book a gig at the Indigo Alley pub in Scarborough. The owner, who was called Ian, had said that he would pay them fifty quid for a one hour session split over two halves and if they wanted to pass a tip jar around during the interval then that was fine by him.

They were driving from their home in Egton to a village called Aislaby, which was close by, where they were going to have their practice session. Iris was very good friends with a farmer's wife called Jane, who she had gone to school with, and they owned and farmed the land very close to the village church. Jane had mentioned that they had a large workshop which wasn't in use at the moment but was fully equipped with electrics and at a remote enough distance so as not to disturb the residents if The Sea Creatures ever wanted to use it for band practice. Iris had practically snapped her hand off at the offer and so here they were on their way to turning up the volume at last. Jane's husband had wanted to charge them an hourly rate for the hire of the premises, but Jane would hear nothing of it, and they all eventually compromised on The Sea Creatures paying a tenner to cover the costs of the electricity used.

Violet had been suffering from toothache now for several days but had bought some extra strong painkillers which seemed to abate the pain and, although she was dealing with it, she knew that she was only putting off the inevitable trip to the dentist. Today however, it gradually seemed to be getting worse and Violet was somehow connecting that fact to the current weather conditions. It had been getting increasingly hot and humid during the day and the thunder clouds had been gathering for a good few hours now, becoming more ominous and menacing as the time went by.

They passed a church on their right and the cenotaph on their left and very shortly after the junction, Iris indicated a right turn and manoeuvred the van through an open wooden gate and then proceeded down a long dusty private road, which was bordered both sides with a barbed wire fence, to a building which was predominantly constructed out of corrugated iron sheeting. There was a side door which was open, but Jane, who was standing there waiting to show them around, had slid back the large front door which would allow them to get their gear inside more easily.

Iris parked the van and they both got out and greeted Jane. It was impossible not to observe the multitude of swallows and house martins that were darting, swooping, and weaving through the air, pursuing the myriad of flying insects that were present in the atmosphere just like a squadron of Spitfires and Hurricanes engaged in a dogfight.

"Nice makeup, Violet," commented Jane with a big smile. "Come on in and I'll show you what's what."

They followed her into the workshop and walked to the far end of the building, passing various items of farm machinery, workbenches, tools and stacks of wooden pallets along the way. Jane turned on the strip-light and pointed out the electricity points. She told them if they needed anything else just to give her a ring as she would be back at the farmhouse, which was only two minutes away. They all walked out of the workshop and Jane asked them if they could close the padlocks on the side and main doors when they left.

"Just snap them shut when you're finished and then give us a ring to say you're leaving."

They both agreed that they would and, as Jane walked up the dirt track back to the farmhouse, Violet and Iris began unloading the equipment into the building.

After half an hour, they were set up and Violet slid the main front door shut. She turned on her Marshall amp and it instantly came to life. It was a great buzz and a relief for them both to finally be able to turn up the volume and for Iris to be able to knock the hell out of the drumkit. The overall sound would be so much more effective and satisfying than their quiet acoustic practices had ever been.

Violet was playing the violin through a set of effects pedals that she operated with her foot and when she turned on the distortion along with the reverb of the amplifier, the sound that she created was powerfully overwhelming and loud enough to wake the dead.

"Why don't we play through the first set, beginning to end, and then have a break?" suggested Iris.

"Whatever you say, honey. Let's do it," replied Violet, who had the setlist taped to the microphone stand in front of her.

Iris counted them in by simultaneously banging her drumsticks together in the air and shouting. "One, two, three, four."

And then the opening staccato notes of Purple Haze by Jimi Hendrix blasted out of the amplifier. Iris joined in with much enthusiasm, and The Sea Creatures first proper loud rehearsal was at last under way.

When they had finished the song, Violet immediately turned around to Iris with a big grin on her face, and the pair burst out laughing.

"That sounded bloody awesome," announced Iris.

"I know," agreed Violet. "Let's crack on." She turned

back to the microphone and said to the imaginary audience. "Good evening, guys, we are The Sea Creatures, and this next song is Rockin' in the Free World by Neil Young. Thank you."

The band launched into their second song and were nearly at the end when Violet noticed a group of people enter the workshop from the side door. They looked like a family, the man leading the way, followed by a woman who was holding a baby in her arms, and she was followed in turn by two young children, a boy and a girl. They walked towards the band and stopped about ten feet short where they continued to observe the performance. Violet was hoping that they had come to listen to the performance and not to complain, as this venue was ideal, and she didn't want to lose it. Violet chose to complete the song, seeing as this was their first 'live' audience, and when they did it was the man who spoke first.

"Will you please turn the music down? It is far too loud, and we are all trying to sleep."

Once again, Violet was struck by the strangeness of the situation. They were obviously locals who were complaining, which was a crying shame and her heart sank at this, but why were they trying to sleep at this time of the day as it was only late afternoon? Violet immediately backed down without argument.

"Yes, of course, we'll turn it down, and I do apologise for any inconvenience. I'm so sorry," Violet promised in a cringing voice.

"Well, just make sure you do or else I will have to complain to a higher authority." And, as the first rumbles of thunder started in the distance outside, the family turned around and headed back to the side door.

"Who the hell are you talking to?" enquired Iris in a confused tone of voice.

Violet spun around to face her. "Them, of course," she said as she pointed behind her with her violin bow.

"Who?" Iris asked again, holding the drumsticks up in a questioning pose.

Violet turned back to see the family exit through the door that they had come in through.

"You must have seen them. There was a family stood right in front of us and the bloke asked me to turn the volume down. They were obviously locals who were complaining."

"I think those painkillers of yours are stronger than you think, girl. There was nobody there."

"You must have been too involved in your drumming to have noticed them. But you must have heard him speak?"

"Nope, only you. I tell you, there was nobody there. Your mind's playing tricks on you, babe. Should we just get on with it?"

"Not until I turn this down a bit. We can't afford to lose this place," said Violet as she walked over to the amplifier. "And you're going to have to play a bit quieter too."

Iris sighed and rolled her eyes. "Whatever," she capitulated, and with that, they finished the first set at a lower volume, although it was by no means quiet.

They were both smoking cigarettes during their midway break as the thunder became perilously louder and obviously closer. The temperature had dropped dramatically, and they could see through the gaps in the main door that it had become eerily dark outside. Suddenly there was a strobe light flash of lightning followed very closely by an enormous clap of thunder.

"Woohoo, we've got our own light show," announced Violet as an onslaught of huge raindrops started to batter against the corrugated iron roof.

"I think we better get on with it," said Iris as she crushed out her cigarette on the concrete floor. "We don't want to be driving home in a flood."

Violet agreed and picked up the electric violin from its stand. As well as doing versions of hard driving rock songs, they had both decided early on that they should put in the odd slower paced ballad type number just to balance out the flavour of the whole set, and it was one of these tunes that they were going to open the second half of the set with and, as the deafening sound of the barrage of rain from above filled the workshop, Violet turned on her amp and announced.

"Welcome back, guys. Here we go again."

"Why don't you try and do some comedy stuff in between songs for a change? You know, just to make it sound a bit more interesting."

Violet slowly turned around to Iris and asked, "What do you want, music and comedy?"

"Well, as an alternative to silence and sadness, yes."

Violet shook her head and flicked Iris the bird before turning back to the mic.

"This song is Lavender by Marillion," she told the

invisible audience, and proceeded to play the opening bars which were normally performed on a keyboard, then she stopped. "Sod it," she said and walked over to the amplifier. "I can hardly hear it with all that bloody racket going on." And as she turned up the volume knob, Iris did a drum roll in agreement on the snare drum.

Violet began again and sang out loud about dreaming of a spark and children running through the rainbows, and when she reached the crescendo beginning of the chorus, where Iris joined in, she had barely managed to sing her favourite line when an almighty explosion rocked the building and the ground beneath them. The flash of light was blinding and the noise from the thunder was deafening.

At the moment that the lightning struck the iron roof of the workshop, the amplifier blew up and the light above them exploded. Violet immediately saw the steel violin strings turn red hot, and smoke come from the body of the instrument. She threw it to the floor in front of her where it broke in two on the unforgiving concrete. She spun around to see Iris just sitting there with a look of bemused terror on her face.

"Oh my God," she said, "we could've been killed. Let's get the hell out of here."

Still in shock, they both began the process of derigging the gear and moving it to the front door. By the time they had piled up the equipment at the door, the storm had moved on, although they could still hear the thunder, and the rain had begun to ease off.

"Let's just get it all in the van and go," suggested

Violet, who was obviously in a distressed state over the destruction of her musical equipment.

They loaded all of the gear into the van, locked the padlocks on the workshop doors and by the time that they had climbed into the front seats, their clothes were soaking wet through but ironically it was then that the rain totally stopped.

"Bloody typical," stated Iris as she pressed the button on her mobile phone to tell Jane what had happened and that they were now leaving. Violet also retrieved her phone from the pocket of her shorts and noticed that she had a text alert. It was from a company of solicitors called White, Grey, Black & Co who were inviting her to the reading of a will down in Kent.

She wasn't in the mood to think about anything like that at the moment and stuffed the phone back in her pocket. Iris talked to Jane as they trundled up the trackway, which was no longer dusty and now had a stream running down the centre of it. She finished the call and then turned the van, which now stank of burnt plastic, left onto the tarmac road on which they had arrived a few hours before, in a totally different mood as to what they were in now.

They drove past the church on their left-hand side and Violet looked at the churchyard which she hadn't taken any notice of on their journey here. The area was quite vast with hundreds of gravestones and monuments. She thought of the family who had visited the workshop that day and what the man had said about sleeping and then what he had threatened with the higher authority.

Maybe the lightning strike was an act of God as a form of punishment for playing too loud. And why hadn't Iris seen or heard them?

She stared at the rows of graves on the other side of the church wall as they drove by and Violet had the enchanting thought that maybe she was lucky enough to have been introduced to a family of ghosts. They passed by the church tower and Violet looked up at the church clock.

"And the clock ticks down and the time moves on," she said out loud.

"You talking to yourself again?" asked Iris.

"Just thinking out loud… I might write a new song, that's all," she said, then put two painkillers in her mouth, and the van continued on its journey down the Egton Road taking The Sea Creatures and their terminally damaged cargo of broken equipment home.

PART 3
THE GATHERING

CHAPTER 1

Andrew Teach returned home with the two bottles and two messages safely stowed away in his shopping trolley. He still lived in the same house that he had been born in, having inherited it when his mother had passed away. The interior of the house, however, was rather more unkempt than when his parents were alive and like most beachcombers, mud larks and field walkers, any empty space had been filled with various curiosities. He actually thought that the inside of his home was even more interesting than Winkies Castle, the museum where he worked.

He took the empty whisky bottle out of his trolley and hid it away in an already overladen cupboard near the television. The note from the Stooges was placed on the mantlepiece, writing-side down, underneath one of the many antique clocks. He retrieved Corky Bottle and made room for him on the side table next to his seat on the sofa.

Then sat down with a sigh and began to re-read the note that had been delivered to him by Corky.

That night he struggled to get to sleep but when he finally did, he had a dream that he was back on the beach, but it was foggy, and he could hardly see more than ten feet in front of himself. All was quiet but then he heard the crunching sound of footsteps on the pebbles which were gradually getting closer. Anxious and frightened at what was going to appear out of the fog, especially after receiving the messages in the bottles, he tried to turn and run but he was rooted to the spot in his sleep paralysis. The image of a person slowly emerged from the fog and stopped. It was a woman. Sandy stared at her and amazingly after all these years he recognised who it was.

"I need your help," she said.

"Queenie, is that really you?" he asked.

"Yes, Sandy. I've received a message about the reading of someone's will, but I have a bad feeling about it, so I want you to come to the place with me. I'll leave the details for you to find in the morning. Please come… it's been too long."

She smiled her beautiful smile then turned and walked back into the fog which quickly disappeared as did the beach, and his dreams went off into random directions.

In the morning he woke up and the dreams vanished from his memory. He got up, dressed and went downstairs. He entered the kitchen and walked to the kettle as he did every morning. Propped up against it was an envelope with Sandy written on it which prompted him to immediately recall the dream of the foggy beach. He opened it up and read the brief note inside.

Please meet me at this address: The George Hotel, 11 High Street, Lydd, Romney Marsh, Kent. They are providing accommodation for the night before the reading of the will which is on the morning of the 1ˢᵗ of November. I'll see you there.

PS. Bring the box with you. I think it's important.

Love from Queenie

XXX

Sandy knew that he had been the only person in the house last night and the note hadn't been there before he'd gone to bed. There was only one person he had ever met in his life who was capable of such a thing and that was Queenie. So, his mind was made up that he'd better start to make the travelling arrangements straight away and, yes, he knew exactly which box Queenie was talking about.

CHAPTER 2

The invitees to the reading of the will had gathered during the course of the day at the George Hotel, all of them making long journeys. It was an old coaching inn whose history stretched back hundreds of years. It used to be a hotbed for smuggling activity with the English Channel so close by. It was often raided by the customs men who wore uniforms and carried flintlock rifles. Eventually the area that was now the dining room was taken over and used as the courthouse where many of the smugglers were tried and hung on the premises. Tommy, the old landlord, had checked them in one by one, given them their room keys and also instructions of where to find their allocated rooms for the night, which were all located on the upper floor of the two-storey building.

It was early in the evening now and pitch black outside with heavy rain lashing against the windows of the small bar room where they were all sitting. They were the only people in the room which had a roaring open log fire with a black cat curled up on a chair by the side of it. Ian Drago and Charlie Clementine were together at the bar, seated on high stools, excitedly chatting to each other about the almost certain probability that they were twins.

Not just because of their striking similarity in appearance but also the fact that the back stories they had been told by their respective adopted parents were identical.

"Just like us," Charlie had quipped.

Stanley Blumenthal was standing with his back to the bar, holding a gin and tonic in one hand. He looked at Richard Redman who was sitting on his own at a table, in a corner next to a flashing and bleeping fruit machine. Richard was gazing intensely at his mobile phone, scrolling through whatever it was that he was watching.

"Are you local to these parts, old boy?" Stanley said.

Richard glanced up without smiling and said in a deadpan tone, "No, I'm down here for business." Then promptly returned his attention to his phone.

Obviously, the man did not want to be disturbed so Stanley turned to face the bar, put his glass down and started to make small talk with Tommy who was perched on a high stool on the other side of the bar.

At the opposite end of the room to Richard, Saffron Simpson, Emma Reldin and Violet Mainprize were sitting together chatting about everything and anything. They had already established that the three of them had been invited here for the same reason and were wondering what the outcome would be.

Queenie was sitting on her own near the doorway to the bar, anxiously awaiting the hopeful arrival of Sandy. She too was immersed in her mobile phone but keeping an ear out for any interesting talk from the rest of them. It was then that she heard the sound of the front door of the pub opening and shutting. She looked up from her phone in anticipation and after a few moments a familiar but older face appeared in the doorway. She shot out of her chair and quickly covered the distance between them. Even though the coat he was wearing was soaking wet, she flung her arms around him and gave him a kiss on the cheek.

Immediately the electricity flowed through him and he let go of the handle of the small suitcase that he was wheeling. In one hand he was clutching a carrier bag but nevertheless he still managed to return the embrace. The three women went quiet as they all eyeballed the scene with intense curiosity.

"I'm so glad you've come," Queenie said to Sandy.

"I've missed you," he said in return, choked with emotion.

They released their grip on each other.

"Come and sit down." She grabbed his hand and led him to the table.

He removed his coat and hung it on the chair that was beside the one he was going to sit on but before he could sit, a voice addressed him from behind the bar.

"Are you staying the night, sir?" asked Tommy.

"Yes, that's right," replied Sandy.

"Can I just ask you to sign the visitor's book."

"Of course." He limped to the bar.

The skinny old barman was unshaven with long silver hair which had thinned out so much that he was bald on top. He offered Sandy a pen and pointed to the open registrar in front of him. Sandy was still clutching the carrier bag, so he swapped it from his right hand to his left and filled in the required details, then handed the pen back. The old man swapped it for a key.

"This one's for your room, which is number two upstairs. And I always shut the main front door at midnight. I'm the only one on tonight and so we have no cook, but I have made some sandwiches for a bit later. It's not much but it's better than nothing. The bar has no formal closing time. I shut everything down when the last customer leaves. I don't need much sleep nowadays, you see."

"Okay, thank you," said Sandy.

"My name's Tommy and you should find everything you need in your room. Would you like a drink?"

"No thanks, I'm okay for now." He turned to look at Queenie and pointed to her half empty glass.

She smiled and shook her head.

Sandy went back to the table and sat down opposite Queenie, placing the carrier bag on the chair where his coat was drying out. He was glad that the open fire was giving out plenty of heat which would speed up the process.

"We're next door neighbours again," she smiled. "I'm in number one."

Sandy laughed and what followed was a conversation catching up on past events of their lives and what they were up to at this present time. Sandy learnt that Queenie had stayed in Cornwall and now lived in Plymouth, her adoptive mother and father had died many years ago and she had never been married. She worked as a music critic for the local newspapers and various magazines like the NME and a couple of famous tabloids as well.

"Is that what I think it is?" she asked him, nodding toward the carrier bag.

"Yes, it is."

"Well done."

"But, how on earth did you get that letter to me?"

"Black magic," she replied with wide open eyes, wiggling her fingers in front of her.

They both laughed.

"I've brought it with me, look." He reached over and searched one of the inside pockets in his coat. He took out the envelope and unfolded it.

"Where's my name gone?" The envelope was blank. He quickly removed the contents and to his astonishment, the note was also blank. "What the...?" He looked up at Queenie who was giggling uncontrollably.

"Good trick, eh!" she said.

He shook his head. "You are something else, you really are."

"Oo-la-la, monsieur, you are so kind," she said in a mocking flirty voice.

"Very funny. Look, could you do me a quick favour and help me up the stairs with my stuff so I can ditch it all in the room?"

"Yeah, no probs." She stood up and took the suitcase, Sandy grabbing the coat, which was considerably drier than when he had arrived, taking hold of the plastic bag.

When they left the bar, Emma Reldin who had been eavesdropping on their conversation turned to the other two women and said, "Well, they didn't waste much time, did they?"

Saffron and Violet both laughed.

CHAPTER 3

Queenie led the way up the stairs and turned left at the top. It was one long corridor which stretched in both directions with doors on either side. The floorboards creaked and some of the walls were warped. The whole place had definitely seen better days but that wasn't surprising as it was so old.

They eventually reached the end of the corridor where there was a closed door, with a frosted glass panel on the top half, facing them. Queenie pointed at it.

"That's the shared bathroom and shower room, by the way. Although you should have a sink in yours," she said.

"Charming," said Sandy.

"Before we go into your room, there's something I need to show you in mine." She pulled a set of keys out of her pocket and inserted one of them into the lock of the door which had a number one on it. She opened the door, leaving the case outside and Sandy followed her in.

"There look." She was pointing at the bedside table.

"Bloody hell, I haven't seen that for years. Why did you bring it with you?"

"That's the point, I didn't. It was here when I arrived. My original one got lost years ago."

"But that's crazy. It looks just the same." Sandy was

staring at a tape cassette recorder that Queenie used to bring to the beach all that time ago, it even had patches of dry sand on it.

"That's not the weirdest thing though." She reached out and pressed the play button. Queen blasted out of the speaker and Freddie Mercury started singing Tie Your Mother Down. After a few seconds she pressed stop and the music ceased. She then pressed the eject button and removed the cassette. She held it up to show Sandy. "That's my writing. That's what I wrote on it back in the seventies."

Although Sandy recognised the tape, he was too shocked to speak. Queenie put the cassette back in and picked up the machine. She turned it around and pointed to something on the back.

"There look, it's my initials that I scratched on it."

Sandy looked closely and he could clearly make out 'AS' which obviously stood for Anne Sinclair.

"It's the same radio cassette, Sandy," she said as she placed it back onto the table. "So, what the hell is going on?"

Sandy finally found his voice. "I was hoping you were going to tell me that."

They stood there in silence for a few moments staring at Queenie's machine.

"Come on," she said, "let's put your things away."

They both left the room and Queenie locked the door as Sandy retrieved his set of keys from his pocket. He put the key into the lock of the door that was adjacent to Queenie's and cautiously pushed it open and entered.

He immediately looked at the bedside table but there was only a lamp on top of it. No nasty surprises. Queenie followed behind with the suitcase, Sandy put the plastic bag on the bed and lay his coat over the back of the only chair in the room. He then took the suitcase off her which he also placed on top of the bed.

"Now it's my turn," he said and started to unzip the case. "Do me a favour, Queenie, and shut the door please."

She did so, then turned back to him. When the case was unzipped, he slowly opened the lid and pointed to the contents. Queenie peered inside.

"Oh my God!" She couldn't believe what she was seeing. On the top of his folded clothes lay two bottles side by side.

"It's Corky Bottle," she said in astonishment.

"Yes, I found it on the beach only a few days ago, the same day you came to me in my dream. It found its way home."

"But what's the other one?" she said, pointing to the whisky bottle.

"Here, I'll show you." He searched the other inside pocket of his coat and pulled out the two pieces of paper. He handed her the first one which had the mysterious riddle on it.

"That one was inside Corky. And this one was inside the other which I found at the same time and place," he said as he gave her the second note.

She read it and then slowly looked up at him with an expression of terror on her face.

"Maynard," she whispered.

Sandy nodded in reluctant agreement.

Suddenly there were three quick loud knocks on the outside of the bedroom door. They both spun around to face it and Sandy walked to the door. He slowly opened it and peered outside. There was nobody there. He poked his head out into the corridor and first looked right. It was totally empty. He slowly looked left. Once again, there was nobody there but he noticed that the bathroom door was half open. Maybe someone had just randomly rapped on his door on the way to use the bathroom, but if that were true there had been no squeaking floorboards to indicate anybody walking towards it.

"Hello," Sandy shouted at the open door. "Is there anybody there?" There was no reply.

"What's going on?" Queenie asked from behind.

"I don't know but I'm going to have a look."

"I'll come with you," she said.

Sandy went first and Queenie followed behind him, leaving the bedroom door open. He reached the door and once again asked if anyone was inside but there was no reply. So, he slowly stepped forward and peered inside. Directly in front of the door was the bath and the shower. He looked to the right. There was a toilet at the end of the bath and at the bottom of the small room was a washbasin. There was no one in here, but his jaw dropped when he raised his eyes to the mirror above the basin. Somehow it was all steamed up, but the terrifying thing was what was written on it…

DIE

Queenie looked over his shoulder and saw the message. It must have been freshly done because there were drops of moisture running down from the letters.

"It's started," she whispered.

"Is everything alright?" someone shouted from down the corridor. They both jumped out of their skin and quickly turned in the direction of the voice. It was Tommy, standing at the top of the stairs.

"Yes, yes, everything's fine, thanks, we were just checking out the bathroom."

"Okay, no worries." He raised his hand and began descending the stairs.

"Let's get out of here," said Queenie. She was already halfway to room number two, but Sandy couldn't resist a last glance around the doorframe and when he did the steam on the mirror, along with the word, had vanished.

"What is this crazy shit?" he muttered as he closed the door and headed to his door where Queenie was standing. He took his key out and locked it. "Let's go," he said. "I think we both need a stiff drink."

CHAPTER 4

"The message had gone by the way," Sandy told Queenie on their way downstairs. She looked concerned and stopped walking.

"I can feel a very evil force in this place, and it means to do us all harm," she said. "It's cunning and is capable of taking on different forms and personalities. We have to be very careful from now on. Trust no one."

Sandy nodded and they continued down the stairs.

They entered the bar and Sandy indicated to the empty chair where Queenie had been sitting previously.

"What would you like to drink?" he asked her as she took her seat.

"I'll have a white wine and soda, please. With ice, thanks."

Sandy nodded and made his way to the bar where Tommy was already standing, ready to serve him.

"What can I get you, sir?"

"Can I have a white wine and soda with ice, please, and a pint of Carling. Please."

"No worries." Tommy slowly shuffled off to fix their drinks.

Sandy noticed how stiff and laboured his movements were, probably due to arthritis or something, he thought.

He looked around the bar room. The old man who was previously stood at the bar was now sitting and chatting with the man who was sitting by the fruit machine. The two men on the bar stools were still talking away to each other and then he heard one of the women speak.

"Excuse me." It was Saffron and she was directing her words at Queenie, who looked at her and smiled.

"We were just wondering," continued Saffron, "if you were both here for the reading of the will tomorrow?"

All three women were smiling at her and awaiting her response.

"Yes, we are. That's right," she replied, lying on Sandy's behalf.

"Ahh, we thought so. Everyone in the room is here for the same reason."

"Oh right. I see."

"Did you know Josie White?" asked Emma.

"No, we've never met her. This is the first time we've even heard of her."

"That's the same as everyone here. It's weird, isn't it?" said Emma.

"When you were out of the room, Tommy was telling us all that she lived by herself in a big house just outside the village and her only company was her long serving live-in house maid," Saffron informed her.

"He said that the locals around here thought that she was a witch," added Violet with her eyes wide open.

"And she was well over a hundred years old when she died," said Emma.

Queenie thanked them for the information and the conversation descended into small talk and polite introductions. Sandy had been eavesdropping and had heard everything that had been said.

"That'll be four pounds altogether, please," Tommy said to Sandy.

"Crikey, that's cheap. Especially for down these parts."

"Yeah but it's Happy Hour, you see. In fact, every hour's Happy Hour in this place." And his weathered face broke out into a practically toothless grin.

'I might have to disagree with you on that after what's just happened to us,' Sandy thought to himself, but he just smiled. "That's excellent." He handed Tommy the money then took the drinks and returned to Queenie who told him the names of the other customers as she had been informed by Violet.

"Everyone's here for the reading of the will," she said.

"Right, that's interesting." Sandy raised his glass to Queenie. "Cheers."

"Cheers," she responded and they clinked their glasses together.

Sandy drank a mouthful. "Have you been in touch with Rusty at all?"

"I tried a few times to contact him the same way I contacted you," she said in a lowered tone so no one else could hear, "but I just couldn't get through. It was like I was being blocked."

"So, he won't be coming here then?"

"I guess not."

The rain had been relentless all evening and there was

a sudden flash outside which, after a few seconds, was followed by a long rumble of thunder.

"Well, that's just great," said Violet. "On tonight of all nights."

A few moments after the first rumble of thunder had finished, the main door blew open with a flurry of cold air and a man entered the bar room, heading for the bar. Queenie, who was facing the entrance, looked up and the man instantly stopped walking.

Sandy looked at Queenie who was staring in disbelief. He turned to look and for the second time that night, his jaw dropped.

CHAPTER 5

"What are you two doing here?" the man said.

"We could ask the same of you," said Sandy with a grin.

There was no doubt about it, with his ginger hair and familiar, although aged, features, it was Rusty.

"I'm working down here at the moment, at the nuclear power plant a couple of miles away at Dungeness. I've just moved into new digs today in a house by the side of the church about a hundred yards up the road. I *was* staying at The Captain Howey Hotel in New Romney but my company decided it was too expensive, the tight gits. Anyway I decided pop in here for a pint. What's your excuse?"

"We're here for the reading of a will," said Queenie. "So is everyone else who's here."

"Come and join us," said Sandy, gesturing to the seat where he had previously hung his coat.

"Absolutely. I'll just grab a pint."

Shortly, Rusty returned, removed his wet coat, hung it on the back of the chair and sat down. He shook Sandy's hand and then Queenie's.

"I can't stay long unfortunately because I'm on a six 'til two shift tomorrow. Early start at daft o'clock."

For the next twenty minutes they chatted about what

they had all been up to over the years as the frequency of the lightning flashes increased and the sound of thunder became closer and louder.

"So, where's all the other locals tonight anyway? Do you think the weather's kept them indoors?" asked Sandy.

Rusty laughed. "I think they might already be here."

"What do you mean?" said Queenie.

"Haven't you heard? I was told earlier by the guy in the Spar that this place is haunted, actually it's one of the most haunted pubs in England."

Sandy and Queenie just looked at each other and took a sip of their drinks.

Rusty glanced at the clock on the wall over the bar and sighed. "Well, I'm sorry guys but I have to go. Let's exchange numbers."

They all picked up their mobiles and did exactly that.

"We'll have to meet up again. Sooner rather than later," he said, standing and putting on his now dry coat. He walked to the other side of the table and shook both of their hands. "It's been brilliant to catch up with you. So, I'll say goodnight and… don't forget to breathe!" His eyes lit up and he smiled knowingly at them. "Sweet dreams, guys, have fun and I'll see you later." Rusty turned and left, and as he did so a flash of lightning from outside and an almost simultaneous crack of thunder sounded that practically shook the building.

"I can't believe that he's down here too," Sandy said to Queenie. "What's the chances of that happening?"

"A million to one," replied Queenie who was vacantly

staring out of the window, her mind preoccupied with other thoughts.

CHAPTER 6

"I'll have another pint of that, please, Tommy," said Charlie, pointing to one of the beer pumps.

Tommy got off his stool, took a fresh glass from under the bar and pulled the handle. Only froth came out.

"Dammit!" he exclaimed. "The barrel needs changing. I dread doing it, you know. I'm not getting any younger and it takes me ages."

"I'll do it," volunteered Ian. "I've got my own bar back home, so I know what I'm doing. Where's the cellar?"

"The door is at the back of the staircase," said Tommy, pointing in the general direction of it. "And thank you, I appreciate any help I can get nowadays. Not that there's much of it round here."

"No problem," said Ian as he got off his bar stool and headed toward the stairs.

"Do you need a hand?" offered Charlie.

"No, it's fine. It'll only take a minute," replied Ian.

He reached the door to the cellar and noticed that there was a key in the lock. He turned it and it opened outwards. He soon found the light switch and turned on the lights. He then descended the stairs, but he didn't notice the door gently close behind him. When he reached the cellar floor, he looked around and tried to locate the correct set of barrels. It didn't take him long to identify the two that he had to work on and as he approached, he noticed that there was something propped up on top of one of them. When he reached it, he nearly fell over backwards. He stared at it in disbelief. It was the black and white photograph that the woman, who claimed to be his mother, had given to him.

And that's when the lights went out.

It had been a quarter of an hour since Ian had gone to change the barrel and Charlie was getting a bit concerned. He decided to give him a ring but then he noticed that Ian had left his phone on the bar.

"I think I'd better go and check on him," he said to Tommy as he got off his stool.

When he reached the cellar door, he pushed the handle down, but it wouldn't open. The door was locked. Charlie turned the key and then it opened. It was dark but he soon found the light switch and turned the lights on. Maybe Ian had finished and gone to the loo or something.

"Ian, are you still down there?" Charlie called out. There was no reply, but sounds of someone shuffling around echoed up from the cellar.

Charlie slowly went down the stairs, calling out on the way, "Ian, is that you?"

When he reached the bottom of the stairs, he looked around but there was nobody there.

'Strange,' he thought, and as he turned to go back upstairs, he noticed something that hadn't been there before. It was on the bottom step.

He bent down and picked it up. He couldn't believe what he was looking at. It was the old paper clipping that Max the ghost train owner had shown him.

And then the lights went out... again, but this time the door didn't just close, it slammed shut.

CHAPTER 7

The storm was still raging and it was with another clap of thunder overhead that Richard stood and wandered to the bar.

"Same again?" asked Tommy.

"No, I'll try a pint of that," he said, gesturing to a beer pump.

The landlord took a fresh glass and began pulling on the pump handle that belonged to the barrel that Ian had gone to sort out. The old man didn't bat an eyelid or even comment when the beer flowed out effortlessly. He filled the pint glass and gave it to Richard who paid the two pounds and then put his glass down on the bar.

"I need to go and point Percy at the porcelain," he said to the others and headed off to the toilets that were situated at the far end of the hall past the staircase.

Emma was the next to go to the bar. Tommy got off his stool and slowly made his way down to her.

"What can I get you, my dear?"

"I'll just have another white wine, please."

He poured the wine and placed it in front of her. She gave him a five pound note and he went to the till. When he returned, she put her hand out but Tommy paused as he held out the change. She was surprised when he didn't drop the coins into her palm immediately and so she looked up at him. He was staring straight at her.

"You ladies couldn't do me a favour, could you?"

Emma was a bit taken aback but she replied, "Depends what it is... Why, what do you want?"

"There are sandwiches in the kitchen for everyone. Could you go and fetch them in for me, please? It's my age, I struggle with things nowadays."

"Yeah, sure. Where's the kitchen?"

"Go past the staircase, turn right at the toilets and walk straight ahead. You can't miss it. There are some trays on the kitchen top."

"Okay, no problem." She was still holding out her hand for the change.

"Thank you," said Tommy and he finally let the coins tumble from his hand into Emma's palm. He smiled at her then turned to go back to his stool.

As he did, Emma looked down to examine the change in her hand. She nearly gasped out loud. Along with the pound coins was the military button that she had given back to the soldier at her cottage door. She quickly looked up to say something, but Tommy was already at the other end of the bar with his back to her. She decided though in hindsight it might be best to say nothing at all. She put the coins and the button in a pocket of her jeans and returned to the table to muster the other two for the sandwich collection.

On the way to the kitchen, the thunder and lightning was still relentless in its fury with no sign of abating. They reached the kitchen and entered through the double doors then the three of them just stopped in their tracks.

"Can you smell that?" asked Violet.

"Yeah, bacon," replied Saffron. "Someone's been cooking smoky bacon."

"But Tommy said there was nobody else here tonight!" exclaimed Emma.

They all saw the sandwiches on the side but also noticed a solitary frying pan on the oven hob. They walked forward to inspect it and found the pan to be empty, no bacon, no fat.

Violet hovered her open hand over the top of it. "It's still hot," she said and picked it up by the handle which was warm. "Mind out the way, I'll take it to the sink." She crossed the room and turned on the cold tap, then placed the pan underneath it which immediately hissed and steamed as it was obviously red hot.

"What the hell?" said Emma, who'd noticed that there was a storeroom at the back of the kitchen. "Is there anyone in there?" she shouted out, but there was no reply.

"This is weird," said Violet. "Let's just grab the sarnies and get outta here."

They all agreed and that's what they did.

They exited the kitchen and headed back to the bar, so nobody heard the shuffling of footsteps coming from the storeroom.

While the women had been in the kitchen, Richard had emerged from the Gents' and was walking past the cellar door when he heard three distinctive knocks. He stopped and reached out to grasp the handle. He pressed it down, but the door was locked and there wasn't much he could do as there was no key in the keyhole.

"Is everything alright in there?" he shouted through the door. There was no answer so, after a short pause, he shrugged his shoulders and walked back into the bar. When he got there, he reported what had happened to Tommy.

"It's a very old building," the old man said. "There's always strange noises coming from it."

"But what about those two?" said Richard, gesturing towards the two empty barstools.

"Well, they've obviously changed the barrel. Maybe they've had enough and gone to bed." Tommy didn't appear to be very concerned about the twins' whereabouts and he just carried on drying a glass with a tea towel.

However, Richard was slightly more suspicious. 'Why would you leave your phone on the bar if you'd gone to bed?' he thought.

He looked around for someone to ask but just then the three women entered the room with the trays of sandwiches.

"Ahh, food at last," Stanley blurted out in excitement. "I'm starving."

"We would have brought you all bacon sarnies, but someone's eaten all the bacon," Saffron said, glancing at Tommy. He didn't react, which rattled her. It felt like he was ignoring her on purpose and that he knew a lot more than he was letting on.

CHAPTER 8

Now and again Tommy would come out from behind the bar and put another log on the fire, and sometimes he would disappear into the small back room behind the bar and reappear a few minutes later.

During the course of the evening people drifted in and out of the bar room to go to the toilet, and the cat slept on in total disregard of whatever else was happening.

In the absence of the eavesdroppers, Sandy and Queenie managed to have a brief discussion about what they had witnessed upstairs.

"You're not happy about things, are you?" Sandy said.

"Is it that obvious?" she replied. "Right from the start, I knew there was something odd going on… even from the moment I received the message about the reading of the will."

"What about the writing on the mirror and the knocking on the bedroom door?" asked Sandy.

She frowned. "I can't possibly imagine all that that was done by a living person, and the venom in the message just adds to my concerns. Like I said before, there is evil in this place, we can't trust anyone."

"What do we do?"

"There's nothing we can do at the moment. We just don't know enough."

Everyone else was helping themselves to sandwiches from the trays the women had put on the bar.

Queenie glanced across. "We should grab something to eat. Who knows when we'll get the chance later."

Saffron watched her new acquaintances piling food onto their plates. She wasn't that hungry but picked up a sandwich and looked towards the door, curious to see if there was anyone else in here. Tommy's demeanour had provoked the investigative journalist in her to come to the fore.

"I'm just going to have a mooch around," she said to the others.

"Go for it," Violet replied.

Saffron left the bar and found herself in a hallway with glass panelled doors. Peering through, it looked like they led into a dining room and at the far end she could just see another door which had a sign above it which read:

THE SMUGGLERS' MUSEUM

'More and more curious,' she thought.

She pushed one of the glass doors open and entered the room. There were eight tables, each one draped with a white tablecloth. The tables were set with placemats and cutlery and they all had a candle in the middle to accompany the salt and pepper pots. On one of the walls was a framed tapestry with the slogan:

A meal without wine,
Is like a kiss without a cuddle

She smiled at that and nibbled on her sandwich as she made her way to the museum entrance. The door to the small room was open so she just stepped inside and began to observe the exhibits, moving in a clockwise direction. There were shelves and glass cases packed with interesting artefacts along with detailed descriptions and facts about the way life was in days gone by. In the middle of the room was a central glass display case, and she slowly made her way around as she ate.

She was halfway down the last wall of exhibits, that included mannequins of smugglers and customs men, when she came across a totally different one. It was an old lady dressed in eighteenth century clothes. She read the information notice to learn that it was an effigy of the landlady who had ran the pub when the smuggling activity was at its height. She was found out, tried and hung on this very spot. But the thing that caught Saffron's eye, and caused her to drop her sandwich, was what was pinned to the woman's chest. It was a brooch identical to the one that she had bought in York, an amber canary with two real tail feathers. And it was in perfect condition. She was shocked at the coincidence and just stood there, staring at it. Then she remembered that her brooch had an individual hallmark on the back. Her curiosity got the better of her, so she quickly glanced around the room and then carefully removed the brooch. She turned it over and studied the back.

"Oh my god!" she said, looking down at it. It seemed impossible but it was the same unique hallmark and initials, which surely meant that it had to be exactly the same brooch.

A cold bony hand darted forward and grabbed hold of her wrist. She screamed out loud and dropped the amber canary.

"HOW DARE YOU STEAL MY JEWELLERY!" a shrill voice screamed at her.

Saffron looked up. The old woman had seemingly come to life and was glaring at her with clenched teeth, her eyes wild with anger. Her face was just inches away from Saffron's and it only took a split second for her to react. She shook off the woman's grip and spun around, falling over in her attempt to escape. And as she did so, the loudest thunderclap of the night so far exploded overhead and every light in the building went out.

"ARGHH," she cried out in pain. "My ankle!"

Saffron crawled along the floor in the darkness and behind her she heard the mannequin dismounting from its display plinth.

"Help me..." she screamed out into the darkness as she clawed at the carpet, inching herself away from the terrifying threat behind her. She gasped quick sharp breaths as the panic of the situation flooded her confused mind. "Please don't hurt me, please leave me alone. I wasn't taking your brooch... I've got one just the same... why would I need it?" Saffron pathetically tried to reason with her pursuer.

She had only managed to travel another couple of feet

194

when a terrific bolt of pain shot from her ankle and up her leg as the mannequin's heel crashed down onto her already severely injured foot.

"Please… someone help me," she sobbed into the blackness as the unseen effigy of the old landlady gleefully increased the pressure and twisted her heel into Saffron's broken ankle with the callous cruelty of an experienced torturer.

CHAPTER 9

If it hadn't been for the glow coming from the open fire, the bar room would have been plunged into total darkness. Even so, the surprise of the unexpected power cut still drew instant gasps of shock from the people inside it. The crack of thunder had been so loud that even the cat had jumped off its chair and was now hiding under one of the tables.

"Don't worry, folks," said Tommy, climbing off his stool. "It happens now and again down here on the marsh."

He reached under the bar and pulled out a cardboard box. As he did so, most of the others shook their mobile phones in order to activate their torches.

"I've got plenty of candles in here," he said and set about lighting them and placing them into either holders or onto old saucers, using drops of hot wax to hold the candles in position.

They all joined in placing the candles onto tables and Tommy spaced a few out on the bar.

"I suppose that's the last of the beer then?" Richard asked Tommy as he peered around from the now dark and silent fruit machine.

"Only the electric pumps. The hand pulled stuff will

still be okay, and I've got plenty of spirits. In fact, there's loads of spirits in this place." The old man laughed to himself as he returned to his perch.

One by one the torches on the phones were turned off as the light from the candles and the fire was sufficient enough to provide some semi decent illumination.

Violet sat up suddenly. "Saffron!" she exclaimed. "I'm going to have a look for her."

"Okay," said Emma, "I'll stay here and look after our stuff. Be careful."

Violet took one of the candles from the bar, choosing to save the charge in her mobile phone and walked out. She was unsure of which direction Saffron had gone so she turned left and headed toward the staircase. The flickering candle created dancing shadows on the walls and another flash of lightning lit the whole place up for a second. She passed the stairs and headed to the toilets. She was about to enter the Ladies' when an open doorway on her left caught her attention. There was a sign which said:

GAMES ROOM

Curiosity got the better of her, so she decided to go and explore. Maybe Saffron was in there. She cautiously entered the room and noticed a pool table, devoid of any balls. She walked alongside of it and noticed an old fashioned Wurltizer type jukebox by the wall on the left. The room was quite long with a few tables and chairs at the far end. She was looking that way when another flash of lightning revealed a silhouetted figure walking from one side of the room to the other. She couldn't make out who it was, so she shouted out.

"Saffron, is that you?"

And that's when the candle blew out and the jukebox turned on. The warm glow coming from it provided stark lighting to the immediate area. The sound of a needle being dropped onto a vinyl record came out from the speakers on the walls and the crackling noise soon gave way to the sound of a piano playing. Violet took a step back. It was a song she knew very well... the opening bars to Lavender by Marillion. Fish, the singer, was just about to explain that he was walking in the park when the needle scratched off the record.

Immediately the raucous screaming of Little Richard singing Tutti Frutti filled the room.

As soon as the singing started, Violet jumped back in horror as pool balls started to shoot up vertically from the pockets of the table. They ricocheted off the ceiling and dropped onto the green baize of the pool table. It was like a machine gun going off. When the last ball dropped, the music instantly stopped. Violet watched, then stepped forward as the balls on the table started to roll together. They seemed to be forming letters. When they had all become motionless, she couldn't believe what she was looking at. The word that had being spelt out was:

DIE

She was paralysed with fear. The balls only held their position for a couple of seconds and then as if being potted by a dozen pool players, they all flew into the pockets and disappeared from sight. The juke box turned off and the room fell into darkness. She couldn't even see the doorway that she had come through. From the far end of the room, she could distinctly hear the sound of someone moving towards her.

"It's time for you to meet the 'Higher Authority' just like me and my family did," a man's voice threatened, and the footsteps broke into a run.

She dropped the candle and fumbled for her phone as she took a few steps in the direction that she thought was the exit. Eventually she pulled out her phone and immediately shook it, the torch came on and she bolted for the doorway, then everything went black as she was struck on the head from behind.

CHAPTER 10

Back in the bar room, everyone was oblivious to Violet's plight as the music hadn't travelled that far.

"By Jove, is that the time?" said Stanley, looking at his phone, which was an older model that wasn't equipped with a torch. It was a quarter to eleven already. "Well, I'm afraid I'm going to have to vacate and hit the hay, old boy," he said to Richard, "It's way past my bedtime."

"No problem, I'll see you in the morning," Richard said to the elderly man.

Stanley rose and approached the bar. "Is it alright for me to take one of these?" he asked, pointing to the candles.

"Of course," replied Tommy, reaching inside the cardboard box. He pulled out another two spare candles and a small box of matches. "Take these as well."

He handed them to Stanley who put them in his jacket pocket, taking one of the candle holders and saying goodnight to everyone as he left the room.

He walked down the passageway and slowly climbed the stairs.

"Up the wooden hill to Bedfordshire," he muttered to himself. When he reached the top, he turned right and walked down the corridor. He was in room number seven which was on the opposite side of the hall to Queenie and Sandy's rooms. When he reached it, he unlocked it and entered. He was just about to place the candle holder on his bedside cabinet when he noticed something very odd. It was something that hadn't been there earlier in the day... a small blue willow pattern vase with a bunch of fresh bluebells and forget-me-nots in it.

"How strange," said Stanley. "Especially for this time of the year, totally out of season, but a nice gesture just the same, from whoever put them there." He placed the candle holder next to the vase, closed the door and locked it. He slowly undressed, blew out the candle and sighed as he climbed into bed. Outside, the lightning provided a strobe light effect through the cracks in the curtains.

He lay there staring at the wardrobe, wondering what tomorrow might bring. There was something about that wardrobe that began to strangely unnerve him. It stood there, sentient in the corner of the room and he felt as if it were observing him with a morbid curiosity. So he closed his eyes and then pulled the duvet totally over his head, wishing for the morning to come quickly.

CHAPTER 11

Richard stood up and placed his empty glass on the bar. "That's me done, I'm going up," he said to Tommy.

"And I'm going to lock up," Tommy replied. "There'll be nobody coming or going now, not on a night like this."

They both grabbed a candle holder and left the bar room.

Emma turned to Sandy and Queenie and said, "I'm getting worried about Saffron and Violet. They've being gone too long, but I told them I would look after their handbags and stuff. You couldn't do me a massive favour and just go and have a look?"

"Yeah, no probs," said Queenie. "It's not like we've got much else to do."

"Oh thanks. They can't be that far away," said Emma.

Sandy and Queenie stood and got themselves a candle holder each. They left the bar and went into the foyer.

"Should we try in here first?" asked Sandy, pointing to the dining room.

"A good a place as any," she replied and they both entered through the glass panelled doors as once again the lightning struck outside and the thunder roared across the heavens.

"There's just you and me in here now, puss," Emma said to the cat who was staring at her from under a table. She rubbed her fingers together and said, "Puss, puss, puss," in a gently coaxing tone. The cat left its hiding place and casually walked up to her.

"There's a good kitty," she said, reaching out to stroke it.

The cat was not pleased. It hissed and bared its teeth, then it swiped Emma's hand with a vicious set of claws.

"Ow, you bugger!" Emma shouted out in pain as the cat shot out of the bar room. It had drawn blood and the wounds burnt like fire. She applied a serviette to the back of her hand.

"There was no need for that, you vicious little bastard," she called out.

Richard decided not to climb the stairs to his room straight away but instead to go to the Gents' toilet downstairs, seeing as there were no ensuite facilities in his bedroom. He walked down the passageway, the candle flickering in front of him. As he passed the cellar door, he noticed that there was now a key in the keyhole. He approached it and tried the handle. The door was still locked so he turned the key and opened it. It was pitch black, the candle barely lighting up the staircase.

"Is anyone down there?" he yelled.

There was no answer. Tommy had probably been right that the pair of them had just gone to bed earlier on. Richard shut the door and locked it, leaving the key in its position. The black cat ran past him as he reached the

Gents' toilets and he pushed open the door. He entered the dark room and then went inside one of the two cubicles. The first thing he noticed was a single red rose that was laid across the top of the cistern.

'Nice touch,' he thought as he shut the door behind him and slid the bolt across to lock it. He placed the candle on the floor in front of him then pulled down his trousers and boxers and squatted on the pan.

About a minute or so later, the door to the Gents' creaked open and someone entered the darkness of the toilet block. The door closed behind the person and Richard heard whoever it was walk towards his cubicle. The footsteps stopped outside of the door and then three loud knocks were promptly hammered on it.

"I won't be a minute… Is that you, Tommy?"

There was no reply just another three loud knocks and the door rattled in response.

"Look, whoever you are, there's another cubicle next door to this one, you know."

There were a few seconds of awkward silence and then the banging on the door resumed. This time it wasn't just three knocks but a continuous volley of knocking which became faster, louder and more furious. It even sounded as if the person outside was using two fists. The candle blew out and Richard found himself in total darkness. He started whimpering as the banging reached a heart stopping crescendo and then all hell broke loose as the door of the cubicle flew right off its hinges.

CHAPTER 12

Sandy and Queenie passed through the dining room and entered the museum.

"Wow!" exclaimed Sandy, scanning the room with his candlelight. "Look at all the stuff in here. I wish I'd known earlier."

"Look on the floor over there," said Queenie, indicating to the other side of the small museum.

Sandy looked over and noticed a half-eaten sandwich with its filling scattered around it. He bent down and picked it up then placed it on the glass cabinet in the centre of the room. Meanwhile, Queenie was taking a good look at the mannequins. She noticed that the old woman figure was wearing a very ornate canary shaped brooch.

'Very nice,' she thought to herself.

They continued to walk around, Queenie taking the lead as Sandy was too distracted by the exhibits. When she reached the open storeroom, she stopped and gasped.

"Oh my god. Quick!" she shouted.

Sandy immediately rushed to her side.

There on the floor, Saffron was laid on her back. Her eyes were wide open and glazed with shock, but her body was motionless. Queenie knelt down beside her and placed the candle holder on the floor. As she felt for a pulse, she noticed the pronounced bruising of finger marks on Saffron's neck.

"Can you feel anything?" asked Sandy.

"No, I can't, and she feels cold. Phone for an ambulance."

Sandy quickly put his candle down and got out his mobile phone. He dialled 999 but there was no dialling tone. He tried several times but with no luck.

"There's no signal," he said and tried walking around the museum to see if he could connect but it was no use. "You're gonna have to try," he said to Queenie, so she did the same with her phone but had the same outcome.

"Let's go back to the bar, maybe Tommy's got a landline," she said.

They both grabbed their candles and rushed off to the bar.

When they got there, the place was deserted. Queenie instantly noticed the three unattended handbags where the women had been sitting. 'That's strange,' she thought. 'Emma must have been caught short and dashed to the loo.'

"Tommy, are you there?" she shouted into the back room of the bar. There was no answer, so she opened the hatch on the bar and stepped behind. She looked into what appeared to be a small office and noticed the telephone on the desk which was in front of another door. She picked it up and dialled but once again there was nothing.

"It's no use," she said, "we're totally cut off."

The lightning struck again as the rain continued to lash down outside.

"What are we going to do?" asked Sandy who was sounding more than just a bit worried. "What's going on and where is everybody?"

"I don't know," replied Queenie, "but I know that we're not safe. Let's go and see if Emma's in the Ladies' loos."

"Are you sure? I think we'd be better off waiting for some kind of back up. I mean, it's quite obvious that Saffron hasn't just choked on a sandwich, isn't it?"

"But what if no one comes back here? I'd rather be doing anything than just sitting, waiting for something to happen. So, are you coming or not?" she quizzed him.

"Well, I'm not staying here on my own, so… after you," said Sandy and he let Queenie lead the way.

As they walked cautiously down the passageway past the stairs, the black cat came sprinting past them, its tail all fluffed out in terror. It darted into the bar room.

Queenie stared after it. "Weird."

"Scaredy cat," said Sandy in a quite pathetic attempt to lighten the mood, and he immediately wished that he hadn't said it, his words being more of a reflection of the way that he was feeling rather than a joke.

They reached the Ladies' and Queenie opened the door.

"Are you staying here?" she asked Sandy.

It didn't take long for his reply.

"You're joking, aren't you? You're not leaving me out here on my own. Ladies' or no Ladies'."

They entered the toilets. Sandy stood at the entrance. There was no one in sight.

"Emma, are you in here?" Queenie shouted out but there was no response. "Violet?" Once again nothing. She approached the first of the two cubicles whose doors were both in the closed position and raised her candle to the door. The bolt told her that the cubicle was vacant, so she gently pushed it inwards. It creaked open and it was indeed empty. She went to the next one which once again said vacant, only this time she had to apply a lot more force to gradually start to open it. It slowly creaked and Queenie immediately discovered that this one too was empty.

"There's no one here," said Queenie as she turned to Sandy. "Let's go."

They left the toilets and stood in the hallway.

"I think we should go back to the bar. It doesn't feel safe," Sandy protested.

"What about looking in there first?" Queenie suggested, indicating to the games room.

"I've got a bad feeling. Let's just go back… please," he pleaded.

"Well, you can go back on your own but I'm going to keep looking. It's up to you."

The idea of walking through the dark hotel on his own was terrifying, so, as the thunder clapped again, Sandy agreed to continue.

"Okay, let's go and take a look."

They both reached the doorway just as a bolt of lightning lit up the room. It flashed for a few moments, but it was long enough to illuminate the disturbing sight on top of the pool table.

"Oh shit!" said Queenie.

They slowly approached the table. Lying on top of the green baize was Violet. Her head and face had been brutally battered, she wasn't breathing and was obviously dead. At her feet lay a broken violin which, from the blood and hair on it, was the murder weapon.

Sandy nearly jumped out of his skin when Queenie shouted out to the room. "Is anyone in here?"

Her question was met with silence.

CHAPTER 13

They left the games room and the tragic sight of the young woman's body. Sandy was feeling both shocked and sickened by the two grim discoveries.

"Let's go and check the kitchen," said Queenie, who so far wasn't showing any signs of fear.

"Do we have to?" pleaded Sandy. "Can't we just go back and tell Tommy?"

"It's only there," said Queenie, gesturing to the kitchen doors.

Sandy sighed and reluctantly followed.

"Actually," he said as they passed by the Gents' loo, "I know this isn't the best time but I'm busting for a pee. Will you stand guard out here while I go?"

"Yeah, but don't be long."

He reluctantly entered the toilets, not knowing who or what might be inside, but it was either this or peeing his pants, and the door shut behind him.

It was only a matter of seconds before Queenie heard an ear-piercing scream and the noise of something clattering on the tiled floor of the Gents'. She was about to push the door when it was flung open and Sandy ran out, almost knocking her off her feet.

"What is it?"

"In there." Sandy was breathing in quick gasps. "It's horrible."

"Oh no!" she said as she turned and entered the loo.

"Be careful," warned Sandy but she didn't reply.

The door closed and she immediately saw two candle holders that had been dropped on the floor, one still had its candle in it but one didn't. One of the cubicle doors had been unceremoniously propped up against the wash basin, but the most distressing part of the whole scene was what was inside the damaged cubicle. It was Richard, who had been left in a most degrading position. He was on his knees, his trousers around his ankles and his head pushed inside the toilet bowl.

"Oh my God!" she cried.

She didn't waste any time checking for signs of life. To be honest, she had absolutely no intention of approaching the man. She immediately left the toilets and re-joined Sandy, who'd got his mobile out and turned on the torch.

"That's disgusting," said Queenie when she emerged.

Sandy was shaking. "We have to find a way to call the police."

"I know. Let's get out of here."

They ran together to the front door. Outside, the wind was howling and the rain was coming sideways at the windows. The lightning flashed and the doors were rattling as the weather battered them.

Queenie tugged on the handle. "Damn. It's locked."

Sandy stood rooted to the spot. There was no key. Tommy had gone to lock the doors for the night. He must have taken the key with him.

"We're locked in," Sandy said, voice quivering. "We're trapped."

Queenie shoved him. "We're not giving in, Sandy Britches. Let's go and see if Tommy's back."

When they got back to the bar, it was still deserted, the three handbags still there, and the cat back on its chair although the fire was now just a pile of glowing embers. They walked to the bar office and looked inside. There was nobody in there

"Actually, I've changed my mind, we'll just stay in here for now. Hopefully someone will turn up." She left the office and went back into the bar room.

Sandy went and stood by the silent fruit machine. "I can't believe this is happening. Less than an hour ago those three were still alive. What's going on... and why?"

Queenie shook her head slowly. "I can't work it out, but there's obviously some psychopath in this building and we're trapped. From now on we need to stay together. Whatever happens. Yes?"

Sandy paused for just a second and then in a quiet voice answered, "That's *exactly* what I think."

"Listen," she said, "You grab us some drinks and I'll light some more candles."

Sandy nodded and went behind the bar while Queenie began to rummage around in the cardboard box that was still on the top. He poured a glass of wine for Queenie and managed to pull himself a pint, not his usual tipple, but he really didn't care. It was just a distraction from the horrific reality of what he had witnessed. He finished pulling the pint, when something caught his eye under the bar.

"Well, look what I've found," he said as he bent down.

"What is it?" asked Queenie.

"You'll never guess." He stood up straight and produced a red Monopoly box.

Queenie stopped lighting the candles and said, "Oh God that brings back memories."

"That's not all though," he added in a more sombre tone as he bent down again and placed another object on the bar.

Queenie stared at it for a couple of seconds. "I think someone wants to tell us something."

It was a Ouija board.

After another short pause, Queenie picked it up. "Come on, we have to sit down." She chose a table near the fruit machine away from the bar entrance, but not the dead man's chair.

Sandy picked up the drinks and joined her.

CHAPTER 14

Upstairs in room number seven, Stanley couldn't get to sleep.

"It's no use," he said to himself. "I'll have to try a nightcap… or two. Hopefully the bar's still open."

He sat on the edge of the bed and managed to light the candle. As he did so, he noticed that the flowers were still fresh and looking very pretty. He slowly got dressed in his dressing gown and slippers and picked up the candle holder. He was just about to leave the room when there were three loud knocks from the inside of the wardrobe door. He stood there frozen with terror, unable to speak.

"Stanley, it's me. It's Veronica. Open the door and let me out. I just want to see you one last time."

It was the voice of a young girl. He knew that he must be dreaming but try as he might he just couldn't wake up and the dream would not break.

"Stanley, open the door. Do it now!" The voice was becoming inpatient and the door began to rattle with another series of more desperate knocks.

He spun around to the bedroom door and as he did so he noticed that the bluebells had suddenly all died and that they were now brown and withered. He fumbled to unlock the door as the noise from the wardrobe became unbearable. He finally succeeded and quickly pulled it open. He dashed outside and ran down the corridor as the maniacal laughter of what seemed like some deranged mental patient sounded from inside his room. Stanley was moving so fast to get away from whatever it was that it wasn't long before the candle went out and he was surrounded by darkness.

Downstairs in the bar room, Sandy and Queenie were sitting at the table with the Ouija board. The candles flickered, and the shadows danced. They both had an index finger on the planchette.

Queenie began to speak. "Is there anybody here that means us harm?"

It moved straight away to the top left-hand corner of the board.

YES.

Queenie closed her eyes as she searched for another question.

"Did you used to live here?"

The planchette moved to the opposite corner.

NO.

"Did you die here?"

It moved away but then moved back.

NO.

"Why do you mean us harm?" asked Sandy, his voice shaking.

Y... O... U... K... I... L... L... E... D... M... E...

They both stared at each other, knowing what the next

question had to be, but who dare ask it? It was Queenie who finally spoke.

"What is your name?"

They looked on horrified as the word was spelt out.

M... A... Y... N... A... R... D...

And then they both cried out as the board flipped up in the air with both it and the planchette landing several feet away.

"Oh God, we're in the shit now," said Sandy.

Queenie looked at him with dismay. "We have been since the word go."

Upstairs, Stanley stumbled forward. The candlelight had robbed him of his night vision, so he was in total darkness. He was feeling along the wall on his right-hand side and he had no idea of his bearings. The laughing had stopped but he could feel the presence of someone now stalking him.

"Stanley…" the voice whispered in a sinister menacing tone. "I only want to talk."

He whimpered with fear as he continued on his journey. He had no idea where the staircase was but shortly he came to what he thought must be the shared bathroom door. He pushed it open with an overwhelming sense of panic, stepped inside and managed to slide the bolt across to lock it.

'Thank God,' he thought, his breathing shallow and his heart racing. He backed as far away from the door as he could and stood there in silence. There was a flash of lightning, and it lit up a figure that was somehow inside the room near the door that he had just bolted shut. The figure took a step towards him.

"Stanley," it whispered softly, "I only wanted to talk to you..." and in a heartbeat it covered the distance between them.

CHAPTER 15

When the light had gone out in the cellar, Ian Drago had lost his bearings and had managed to find his way into a tunnel. It was pitch black and he had no source of light with him, so he was inching his way along, one hand feeling the cold damp stone wall and the other held out in front of himself. Now and again he would stop and recoil as he came into contact with unseen spiders' webs, but his biggest fear was that he might come across a staircase or a ledge and be plunged into an uncontrollable freefall. If that were to happen, he had no form of communication and no way of summoning help and so he would surely perish if he sustained a crippling injury.

He had been down here for quite some time now and had discovered that this wasn't just one tunnel but a network of connecting tunnels with numerous junctions and crossroads and now he was completely lost, all sense of direction having long since deserted him. What he didn't know was that the tunnels he was unwillingly being forced to explore had originally being created hundreds of years ago by the smuggling community, thus providing an invaluable route by which they could transport their contraband easily and effectively from various locations without being detected.

He stopped shuffling forward and shouted out into the darkness. "Hello. Is there anybody down here?"

The only reply was a distant lonely echo. "...*anybody down here?*"

He tried again. "Hello. Can anybody hear me?"

"... *hear me?*" said the reply of his own concerned voice.

He was feeling desperate now and close to tears but before he had a chance to continue on his journey, a voice called back from somewhere up the tunnel in front of him.

"Ian, is that you?"

It was the voice of a woman. He was stunned into silence. Who could it be down here in the dark? Someone who knew him by the sound of it.

"Ian, is it you? Are you my Ian?"

'My' Ian? That was even crazier.

"I've come to rescue you. I promised I'd never leave you."

The voice didn't sound threatening, but it did sound strangely familiar, as if he had heard it before somewhere. Then he heard the unmistakeable sound of footsteps heading towards him.

"Yes, it's me, it's Ian, but who are you?" he shouted out.

"... *who are you?*" came the haunting sound of his echo, however there was no other reply and the footsteps kept getting closer and closer until they finally stopped right in front of him.

He flailed his arms around wildly trying to feel for the mystery person, but it was the invisible stranger who grabbed him by the wrists and her hands were stone cold. Ian shrieked in terror.

"Don't hurt me," he wailed. "Leave me alone."

"I never really left you alone," said the woman, "but now it's time for me to take you back home… where you came from." Her voice had taken on a more menacing tone and Ian was petrified. She suddenly released her grip on his wrists, but Ian had no time to react as immediately her icy grip returned, only this time it was around his neck.

Before she managed to strengthen her hold, Ian let out a deafening scream of terror.

When the cellar light had gone out, after his initial panic, Charlie had managed to activate his phone light and had tried to open the door at the top of the stairs which had somehow been locked shut. After several attempts of banging and shouting with no response, he descended back to the cellar where he'd found what he hoped would be an alternative escape route. At first, with the luxury of the torchlight, he made good progress into the tunnel but then he suddenly stopped. He had just had a brainwave and he didn't know why he hadn't thought of it before. He remembered that Ian's phone had been left on the bar so all that he had to do was call it and hopefully, if the connection was working from down here, someone would answer.

It was simple.

He fumbled to find the contact number, scrolling frantically, and was about to press the number with relief when the screen went blank. He stared at it. It had been on over half charge, he was sure. But now nothing, even trying to turn it on and off. Nothing.

He was stuck down here in the darkness, trapped like a lobster in a lobster pot, easy to get into but seemingly impossible to get out of.

He almost fell over when he heard the scream far away in the distance. It was coming from somewhere ahead.

"Ian, is that you? Is that you, Ian?" he shouted.

"...is that you, Ian?" the tunnel echoed back to him.

Charlie reluctantly began to edge forward, and in no time found himself in exactly the same predicament as his twin brother had, lost and confused, but he had no option other than to carry on and try to find a way out of this foreboding maze of cold and dark. After a few minutes of slow progress, he stopped as he became aware of footsteps following him, which seemed to be getting closer.

"Ian? Ian?" he asked into the abyss.

"...Ian? Ian?" came the reply.

He was trembling as the footsteps came right up to him and stopped a couple of feet away.

"I'm not your brother, Charlie..." whispered the gentle voice of a woman. There was a split-second pause then she thrust her face inches in front of his and screamed, "I'M YOUR MOTHER."

Miraculously illuminated somehow from underneath, the contorted image of the woman glowered at him then she leapt forward and bundled him to the floor.

Unlike Ian's scream before him, nobody had heard Charlie's screaming from deep down in the underground tunnels which had now become an underground crypt.

CHAPTER 16

Upstairs, Sandy and Queenie were sitting, staring at the upturned Ouija board on the bar room floor.

"You're not going to like this," she said to him without shifting her gaze.

"What is it?" He turned to her with an alarmed expression.

She slowly turned to him. "We're going to have to fetch the box." She gestured to the ceiling with her eyes.

"What? Leave here and go up there? You haven't forgot that there's a killer on the loose, have you?"

"No, but now it's time to bring it down."

"Why can't we stay up there with it?"

"Because I think it'll be safer for us down here. Besides we've got the added light from the fire." She rose from the table and walked to the fireplace.

The black cat was still curled up asleep on the chair, strangely enough it hadn't been startled at all by the sudden flight of the board through the air.

Queenie picked up a log from the pile and, using the iron tongs, she placed it gently on top of the glowing embers. She put the tongs down and reached out slowly to stroke the cat's black fur. As she did so, the cat just lay there and started purring contently.

Queenie straightened up and looked at Sandy. "Come on. Let's get it over with. Don't forget your phone and we'll take a candle each with us. Oh! And also, we'll take these."

Sandy joined her by the fire as she handed him a metal poker, taking the tongs for herself. They then grabbed a candle each then, as the lightning flashed and the thunder cracked, they left the sanctuary of the bar room.

They climbed the creaking stairs by flickering candlelight, their weapons clenched tightly in their hands. Queenie led the way with Sandy following close behind and they both carefully scanned the surroundings like soldiers on patrol. They reached the top and cautiously approached Sandy's room.

"Give me the key," said Queenie, and he did so.

"Actually," he said looking in the direction of the bathroom. "I still haven't gone to the loo. It's no use... I'm gonna have to go."

"Well, be quick," said Queenie as she turned the key in the lock. "And be careful," she added.

Sandy gulped, and totally aware of what had happened before with the mirror, he advanced to the darkened bathroom as Queenie slowly opened the door of room number two and entered.

He reached out his hand and gently pushed the bathroom door which creaked open on its hinges. He walked forward and illuminated the room with his candle.

Queenie moved towards the white plastic bag and reached out for it just as a blood curdling scream rang out from the direction of the bathroom. She grabbed the bag and spun around to the doorway. Sandy was racing past, his candle extinguished.

"Just run, Queenie. We gotta get out of here," he shouted.

She wasted no time and ran out of the room without bothering to close the door or remove the key.

"What is it?" she yelled as they both bolted down the corridor.

"That old man, Stanley…" he gasped. "Face down in a bath full of water. He's dead."

"Oh God."

When they were inside the bar, Queenie put the bag on the table by the fruit machine and as they struggled to get their breath back, it was Sandy who spoke.

"I don't mean to sound awful. But I still haven't managed to go for that pee yet. So please excuse me. I'm going to find an empty bottle, or two, or three. Before there's a nasty accident." He went behind the bar. "Even better, an ice bucket." He picked it up and went into the office while Queenie put another two logs on the now rekindled fire and lit some more candles.

CHAPTER 17

"God, that feels better," said Sandy as he joined Queenie. He noticed that she had picked up the Ouija board and placed it on the top of the bar.

"Who do you think's behind all of this?" he asked her.

"I can't work it out," she said. "We know that there's definitely supernatural and evil forces present here, just look at the mirror and the Ouija board. And we know that there's four people dead but there's also four people unaccounted for. I mean, where's Tommy disappeared to? Has he copped it as well? And why has Emma left those handbags unattended for so long?"

"And what about those two that were sat at the bar?"

"Maybe they're all dead? Maybe it's some random lunatic who has been hiding in the hotel somewhere and nobody knew? Maybe there's just us two left? I don't know, but I do know one thing for sure though."

"What's that?" asked Sandy.

"We're not moving from here until it's daylight. Hopefully we can find a key for the front doors and escape." Queenie pointed to the plastic bag. "Can you take it out? I don't like to touch it. It gives me the creeps."

Sandy reached inside as Queenie held the bag and he pulled out the small antique treasure chest.

"Do you remember the day that I gave you that?" asked Queenie.

"I'll never forget it. I think about it all the time," he replied in a solemn tone. "You said that it was a family heirloom that your birth mother had given to you, and it was the only thing of any real value that you had. You said that you wanted me to look after it and keep it as something to remember you by." He wiped away a tear from the corner of his eye.

"Yeah, that's right," nodded Queenie.

"But I've never being able to prise it open. I've often wondered what's in it."

"I guess some things just aren't supposed to be opened up, a bit like old wounds or something."

"But why did you want it brought here?" asked Sandy.

She shrugged her shoulders and said, "I thought that seeing as it had family connections, and this was the reading of a family will that it might be important."

"Maybe…" said Sandy. "The funny thing is, I didn't see those two small initials carved into the back of it at first and five years later after you'd given it to me, when that film ET came out, I thought that he might be in the box. I thought there might have even been a phone in there too."

There was a slight pause and then they both laughed.

"You always were a silly sod," said Queenie as she playfully swiped his shoulder.

"Should we have another drink?" suggested Sandy. "This is going to be a long, long night."

Just as he was about to rise from the table Queenie grabbed his arm.

"Be quiet," she whispered. "There's somebody coming down the stairs."

Sure enough, they could hear the slow methodical sound of footsteps and the staircase creaking in unison. Sandy and Queenie stood up in silence, brandishing their weapons and preparing to face whoever was about to appear at the doorway.

CHAPTER 18

Through the bar room entrance, Sandy and Queenie could see the shadows dancing around in the foyer as someone approached and it wasn't long before the individual appeared. The gnarled old figure of the landlord came into view. He was carrying a lantern that contained a burning candle and he stopped at the doorway.

"Tommy, where have you been? Do you know what's going on?" asked Queenie.

He didn't reply. He just stood there, staring at the chest on the table. He slowly raised his arm and pointed at it.

"There it is. Our chest. It was you that had it." He looked over at Queenie and spoke with an accusing tone. "It was stolen from us a long time ago but now it's back. Where it belongs."

"What do you mean? Your chest?" asked Queenie. "It was given to me years ago. I had it brought here because it's a family heirloom and I thought there was a chance that it might be included in the reading of the will tomorrow."

Tommy laughed. "There'll be no reading of any will tomorrow. That was all a con just to get you all here. We knew that one of you lot must have it so we went ahead with our plan on the assumption that whoever had it would bring it, and you, my dear, have fit the bill perfectly. Well done, now give it back to me."

"You're not making any sense," Sandy said. "Who's the we? Who *are* you?"

"Fair enough, I'll tell you. My name is Thomas White, and my sister is called Josie. We both left this world many years ago, but now we've come back to right a wrong. As I said earlier this evening, people around here thought that my sister was a witch. Well, she was… in fact, she still is, but no, she didn't live in a big house, she used to be the landlady of this place and you've already met her although you don't know it. We acquired that chest a long time ago. It was hidden down in the cellar along with a cargo of rum from the Caribbean and when I saw it, I took a fancy to it, so it became ours, finders keepers and all that. The only problem was it didn't have a key and try as I might, I couldn't open it, so I arranged for the local blacksmith to have a go. The night before I was due to take it to the forge, it went missing. Someone had stolen it and that someone disappeared in an accident never to be seen again. It was our own brother who took it and he drowned shortly afterwards when a fishing boat he was on sank without trace during one stormy night. Josie and me reckoned that his wife had knowledge of the chest and when she did a moonlight flit with their children a couple of days after he drowned we got even more suspicious. So we tracked down all of his descendants and invited you all here. But the chest is here now, and we want it back."

"Why is it so important?" asked Sandy. "It's just an empty box."

"Oh no, it's not," said Tommy. "When I found the chest in the cellar, it was hidden in a sack along with a note. It said that whoever is in possession of the chest and manages to open it will inherit riches beyond their wildest dreams but beware anyone who tries to cause harm to the true owner as it is guarded by powers from beyond this world."

The lightning flashed and the thunder rumbled.

"What did you mean by we've already met your sister?" asked Queenie.

Tommy grinned his macabre grin. "I'll tell her to come and join us." He turned towards the dining room. "Josie, come on out and say hello to our guests."

The doors of the dining room opened of their own accord and stayed in that position. Sandy and Queenie became aware of a shuffling noise in the darkened room which was coming from the direction of the Smugglers' Museum. They strained to see anything but whoever was in there was getting closer. The only light being cast was the ambient light from Tommy's lantern which he held aloft providing stark illumination to the foyer. They held their breath as the thing from the dining room slowly appeared in the glow of the lantern. It was walking stiffly.

"Oh, my god!" gasped Queenie. "It's alive."

The figure approached Tommy and stood by his side.

"Let me introduce my sister... Josie White," said Tommy.

Sandy was appalled. "Jesus Christ, this is horrific."

The old lady mannequin from the museum had

somehow become animated and had made its way to the bar room. Queenie recognised it straight away by the amber brooch it was wearing.

"Give us our chest back," it snarled as the black cat jumped from its chair and began to rub itself around Josie White's ankles, purring with pleasure.

"You can have the damn thing back but just answer us one question," said Queenie. "Who the hell has being going around murdering people?"

Tommy paused before he answered. "I was approached by a young man who got wind of the scheme I was drawing up as he had a keen interest in certain individuals who would be attending. It was nothing to do with our chest, but I wouldn't have been able to send out all of the correspondence about the will by myself, so I needed some help. I knew what his intentions were, so I told him that I didn't want any living witnesses to any kind of misdemeanour on my property. It was a simple deal really, a case of if one gets it then everyone gets it, and nobody ever leaves. It's a big cellar down there, you know."

"You still haven't told us who it is yet. So, who is it?" Queenie demanded.

Tommy paused again before speaking.

"Okay then. It's time for the big appearance of tonight's special guest. Come out of the shadows, my friend."

Purposeful but steady footsteps could be heard in the darkened foyer and it wasn't long before another figure emerged from out of the gloom to stand beside Tommy and the effigy of Josie White.

Sandy and Queenie's jaws both dropped in unison their

eyes wide open, Queenie had both of her hands over her mouth and neither could speak.

There in front of them stood their old friend Rusty. It was hard to tell in the dim light, but his face appeared as white as a sheet, his eyes blank and unblinking. He turned to the side and reached into his large coat.

"I've brought you both a present," he said, although it didn't sound like Rusty. He then spun around and lobbed something towards them. It was the size of a football and it landed with a thud on the table in front of the one that they were standing beside. They both got splattered with drops of liquid and Queenie let out a scream as Sandy recoiled in horror. Looking back at them was the severed head of Emma Reldin. Reacting to their obvious revulsion, Rusty laughed a crazy maniacal laugh.

"Special delivery for Long John and the Bitch Witch."

As soon as he spoke, the penny dropped, it wasn't Rusty at all.

"Maynard. What have you done to Rusty?" Sandy shouted at him.

"Simple really. I just possessed his body. I'm really good at imitating other people as you rightly guessed." And he laughed that revolting laugh again. They couldn't believe that the person before them was their friend Rusty but they were actually communicating with the ghost of Maynard.

"It's been quite fun actually, dealing with the others. Just like snuffing out a rainbow, like wiping it from the sky." He then thrust his hands into his deep side pockets and pulled out a claw hammer and a long-bladed kitchen knife. "And now it's your turn to join them."

"Would you like to have your fun with them now and then we'll just take the box?" Tommy said to Maynard.

"There's really only one answer to that," laughed Maynard.

It's strange but sometimes the most brilliant spark of inspiration comes from being caught in the most traumatic of situations, and that's exactly what happened to Sandy. Recalling the message that was inside Corky Bottle regarding that he 'now had the answer', he felt in his pocket and he pulled out the key that he had found on the beach. He fumbled it at the keyhole in the front of the chest and to his relief it went straight in. He remembered putting it in his jeans pocket but had forgotten all about it.

It was like a Mexican stand-off, nobody knowing whether the key would turn or not. After a few seconds of high tension, it was Tommy who broke the silence.

"Ahh, to hell with it! Kill them, Maynard. I want that chest."

Without hesitation Maynard moved forward.

Queenie stood her ground, brandishing the fire tongs and ready to strike out at the first opportunity, which was quite unnerving as it felt like she would be striking her old friend Rusty.

The key wouldn't turn.

Sandy frantically rattled it back and forth. Maynard was only a few paces away now when miraculously the key turned, and the lid of the chest flew open with a deafening roar of cannon fire. It was such a violent motion that it knocked both Sandy and Queenie off their feet. Maynard stopped in his tracks as immediately a billowing thick cloud of black smoke, like a rolling thunder cloud, erupted from the small chest. This was accompanied with the ear-piercing scream of a thousand banshees. In a matter of seconds, the entire room was filled with the smoke and the stench of burning gunpowder. Then the screaming stopped, and all was silent.

CHAPTER 19

Sandy and Queenie crawled under the table and cowered there as the smoke slowly began to clear and the smell of gunpowder gave way to the stench of dead crabs and rotting fish. They looked on from underneath their shelter as the dense fog turned into a thin mist which revealed the legs of numerous people clad in black leather boots decorated with ornate silver buckles.

Sandy craned his neck so that he could get a better view and what he saw astounded him.

The room was full of pirates. They were a menacing bunch of individuals whose reputations of criminality were etched into their scarred and weathered faces. Directly in front of the table that they were hiding underneath towered a well-built man with a plaited ponytail, and from this angle Sandy could just about make out that he was wearing a tricorn hat.

"Nobody ever steals from Blackbeard and gets away with it," the man bellowed.

At the other end of the room, Tommy and Josie were rooted to the spot surrounded by hardened buccaneers. At Blackbeard's feet, the pitiful shell of Rusty was on its knees, head bowed.

Blackbeard looked down. "You again, trying to hurt

my own blood kin. I know you're in there, now it's time for you to show yourself..." He roared at the top of his voice, "SHOW YOURSELF."

Rusty's body slumped backward as a grey mist spiralled upwards from the top of his head. The mist then transformed into the figure of Maynard which stood before Blackbeard, his face twisted with terror.

"I thought you would have learnt your lesson from last time. Well, this will be your last time," said Blackbeard as he drew his cutlass and in one decisive side swipe decapitated Maynard's ghostly head. Maynard instantly vanished. "Now finish off those two thieving bastards." Blackbeard pointed his cutlass at Tommy and Josie.

"No, no, please, I can explain," begged Tommy, but it was too late as the pirates set about them with an energetic fervour, and Sandy thought it was quite bizarre to watch the mannequin of Josie White being smashed to pieces with her own detached limbs. During the maelstrom of violence, Rusty managed to stagger to his feet and he stumbled out of the bar room.

Blackbeard turned towards the table that Sandy and Queenie were hid under and banged on it with the hilt of his cutlass.

"You two can come out now," he said.

They both slowly emerged and stood up.

"You..." the pirate said in a low threatening growl, pointing at Queenie, "you be descended from those evil bastards..." He levelled his cutlass at her and for a hideous moment Sandy thought he was going to attack but Blackbeard laughed. "But I sense good in you. You can live." He then turned to Sandy, "You be the rightful owner of this chest. It were gifted to me hundreds of years ago by a Voodoo queen in exchange for her son's life. We caught him trying to steal bread from the galley of our ship when we were moored up in Haiti, but I lost it when it got misplaced in a consignment of rum which was destined for here. She told that me that only the real owner could ever be the one to open it and from now on your life will be filled with untold treasures. We are going to go back into the Deadman's Chest now so keep it safe and we will always be there to protect you."

"Yes, of course," said Sandy, his voice faltering with adrenaline.

"Right, you lot, it's time to get back on board," Blackbeard shouted to his crew.

They all advanced towards the chest and one by one they were quickly sucked inside by an invisible vortex. The last one to enter was Blackbeard.

"Thank you," shouted Queenie as he disappeared from view.

When he was gone, the lid slammed shut and the key turned in the lock and ejected itself from the keyhole, Sandy grabbed it immediately and stuffed it back into his pocket.

CHAPTER 20

They looked around at the scene in front of them and Sandy quickly put the chest back into the carrier bag. The mannequin of Josie White had been totally smashed to pieces and the only trace left of Tommy was the broken lantern lying on the floor.

"Have you noticed something?" asked Queenie.

"I've noticed a lot of things," replied Sandy.

"No, outside. The rain's stopped. I've got a strong feeling that things have changed, things have shifted. Come with me."

It was too early to process the immensity of it all so they left the bar room and Queenie tried the front doors. The doors opened and it was immediately apparent that the storm had passed by. They both looked outside, and the pavements and roads were still wet, the rain cascading out of blocked roof gutters but up in the sky the clouds had broken up and were now scudding along, illuminated by a full moon.

"Right, let's wedge these open so they can't shut on us," said Queenie, and so they kicked the door wedges into place.

"What now?" asked Sandy.

"We have to get out of here and find the police station,

but first we're going to get our gear from upstairs," she said.

"Oh god, but there's still no lights on, there's no power. I hate it up there," protested Sandy.

"Look, I've got stuff up there that I need and so do you. A warm coat for a start and the keys to my apartment."

Sandy reluctantly agreed and they both activated their phone torches. Up the creaky stairs they went once more. They cautiously moved down the corridor being totally aware that this might not be over yet.

Sandy's door was still open, the key still in the lock. They both entered together and the first thing that they noticed was that the floor, the bed and the table were covered with shards of shattered glass.

"Oh no, Corky Bottle's been done in as well," said Sandy.

"Just get your stuff," said Queenie.

Sandy walked forward, crunching on the glass. He zipped up his case and grabbed his bag.

"Let's go," he said and they exited the room.

Queenie already had her key in her hand and quickly opened the door to room number one. They stepped inside.

"Oh no!" she said in a tone of despair.

"What is it?" said Sandy, but Queenie just pointed. It was her beloved tape recorder smashed to pieces. There were bits of plastic, transistors, wires and feet of unwound cassette tape littering the room.

"Let's just get out of this place," he sighed.

Queenie retrieved her belongings and they left the

room. They advanced down the dimly lit corridor and as they did so, the door of room number one slammed shut with an incredible bang, closely followed by the door of room number two.

"Do you ever get the feeling that you're not welcome?" quipped Sandy as they both doubled their pace. And then every door that they passed started with furious loud banging and knocking noises. It was as if they were going to be shook off their hinges. Without any encouragement they both broke into a run and soon found themselves down the stairs and outside on the damp pavement. The streetlights were still not working, and so the only light being provided was by the moon above.

"This way," Queenie said.

"Where are we going?" asked Sandy.

"There's a twenty-four hour taxi place just down here. The driver pointed it out when he dropped me off yesterday. There's bound to be somebody in there and we'll get a lift to the police station."

As they walked down the street, they noticed the amount of boarded up shops and offices that there were.

"Bloody hell, will you look at that." Queenie pointed across the street to an abandoned boarded up office.

Sandy was just able to make out the writing on the sign that hung outside: *White, Grey, Black & Co. Solicitors*.

"That's where my invitation to the will reading came from."

"God, it looks like it hasn't been open for donkey's years. Keep walking."

They soon found themselves outside a small portacabin

that looked inhabited, a flickering light showing through the window.

"I think we're in luck," said Sandy as he opened the door.

Inside there were two men, one sat behind a desk which had two lit candles on it and one who looked asleep sat in a chair beside the desk.

"Hi," said Queenie. "We need a taxi to the police station please."

The man behind the desk looked surprised. "Sure. You're not in any trouble, are you?"

"No," they both replied in unison.

The man didn't look convinced but nevertheless he woke the driver and gave him instructions to give the two a lift to the police station.

It wasn't long before Sandy and Queenie found themselves sitting in the back of the car being driven back in the direction from where they had just walked.

"There's a lot of boarded up shops around here," said Sandy to the driver.

"It's the recession, man," he replied. "Take this place for example." He was pointing forward to The George Hotel that they were just about to pass. "It used to be bouncing. So sad."

Sandy and Queenie frowned at each other in puzzlement and then when the taxi drew level with the building, they both just stared at the sight that they were driving past. The George Hotel's windows, and front doors were totally boarded up and red graffiti adorned the flaking whitewashed walls.

"Yeah, it's been standing empty for about twelve or thirteen years now. Nobody wants to buy the place. Most people think it's haunted, but I don't believe in all that rubbish," said the driver.

"But…" began Sandy.

Queenie immediately put one of her index fingers to his lips, her eyes wide in a gesture that basically meant shut up.

"Actually," said Queenie, "the police station can wait until tomorrow and it is the early hours of the morning, it's not that important."

The driver glanced back at her in his rear-view mirror with a surprised look in his eyes.

"Yeah," she said, "it's just I've lost my phone. I'll sort it when I get back home. Can you take us to the train station instead, please?"

"Okay, you're the boss," said the driver and he indicated to make a diverted turning from his original planned route.

Sandy and Queenie both stood together in silence in front of a stationary train on platform three. They had checked their individual departure times, and this was Sandy's train, Queenie's was due to arrive twenty minutes later. Neither of them were in a rush to speak, and neither of them were in a rush to say goodbye. Queenie turned to Sandy and cleared her throat.

"Look, I've being thinking…"

Sandy's eyes widened in cautious expectation.

"I've got quite a bit of downtime at the moment,"

she said, "and, well, if it's alright with you… well, maybe I could come and stop at yours for a while… if that's okay… What do you think? Just for a few days?"

"Queenie, that would be great, and you can stay as long as you want to." He held out his hand, Queenie took it and with the familiar tingling sensation running through him, they boarded the train together.

Immediately following the raucous scene in the bar room at The George Hotel, Rusty had hidden in the dining room for a short while before trying the front doors and then, finding them unlocked, he escaped out of the building and, taking a right, he had ran up the road back to the safety of his digs, wondering what the hell had just gone on.

Queenie spent a full week living with Sandy at his house in Marske and they came to a mutual agreement… because they were so happy together, they would make it a permanent arrangement. Queenie left her apartment in Plymouth and made a smooth transition to her new life in the North East.

EPILOGUE

It was now July of the following year and the three Believers were often in touch with each other on the group chat that Rusty had set up, although what happened that night in Kent was never spoken of. Sandy was sitting next to Queenie on the wooden bench outside of their home. It overlooked the beach and the sea, and the weather was glorious. There wasn't a cloud in the sky and the sun beat down on the pair of them and the beautiful view that they were enjoying together. A black cat jumped up onto Queenie's lap and settled down as she gently stroked it. The cat was a stray that now lived with them. It had turned up shortly after Queenie had moved in and she had named him George.

In the distance, on the beach, they were looking at three children, maybe nine or ten years old who were sitting on a picnic blanket, two boys and one girl. As they looked on, a tuneful sound was carried to them on the salty onshore breeze. It sounded quiet from this far away, but it was still audible, Elton and Kiki were once again singing Don't Go Breaking My Heart. Queenie put her hand on Sandy's and the hairs stood up on the back of his neck with the electric feeling that she generated.

"Weird, isn't it?" he said, "That could be us down there… years ago."

"Maybe it is!" Queenie replied with a wry grin. "Sometimes things come back forever, you know."

"I'm so glad that's true." He squeezed her hand tightly.

"It's good to be home again."

"It's good to have you back. I've being lonely for so long," Sandy admitted.

"What kept you going all this time?" she asked.

"Pretty simple really, it was something that you said to me a long time ago."

"What was it?"

"Well, basically I just never forgot to breathe!"

She thought about it for a bit and then they both burst out laughing. It was at that moment when several things came into sharp focus for Sandy. As he sat there watching Queenie laugh, he finally solved the riddle that Corky Bottle had delivered to him. He had found the answer when he found the key to the chest on the beach and it turned out to be the key to happiness. As his mother had said that Sunday around the dinner table many years ago, 'The key to happiness doesn't always have to involve money,' and the untold treasures that the chest had bestowed upon him were simply the here and now being with Queenie and the fact that he wasn't questioning life anymore. They reached out to the small table in front of them, picked up their glasses of Dandelion and Burdock and raised them in a toast.

"To the future, to the past, but mostly to the present," said Sandy.

Queenie nodded in agreement, they both chinked their glasses and swallowed a mouthful of fizziness.

"And by the way... I love you too," he added.

(IT'S NEVER TOO LATE!)

•

A few days after the incident at The George Hotel, seven separate missing persons investigations had been launched by the police. Although seven in a short space of time was unusual, it is not uncommon for people to go missing and the stories received sparse media coverage.

It wouldn't be until the hotel was purchased by the new owners two years later, and the contract workers entered the building for the first time, that a few macabre discoveries would lead to a whole new can of worms being opened up.